4/72 II
4.79

Exiled from Earth

Other books by Ben Bova

THE DUELING MACHINE

ESCAPE!

GIANTS OF THE ANIMAL WORLD

IN QUEST OF QUASARS

THE MILKY WAY GALAXY

OUT OF THE SUN

PLANETS, LIFE AND LGM

THE STAR CONQUERORS

STAR WATCHMAN

THE STORY OF REPTILES

THE USES OF SPACE

THE WEATHERMAKERS

Ben Bova

Exiled from Earth

E. P. Dutton & Co., Inc.   New York

Published simultaneously in Canada by Clarke, Irwin & Company Limited, Toronto and Vancouver

SBN: 0-525-29425-2
Library of Congress Catalog Card Number: 74-133120

Designed by Dorothea von Elbe
Printed in the U.S.A.
First Edition

In alphabetical order:
To Gordon R. Dickson and Harlan Ellison
with thanks and *caritas*.

Chapter 1

The General Chairman paced across the soft carpeting of his office, hands clasped behind his slightly stooped back. He stopped at the wide sweep of windows that overlooked the city.

There was little of Old Messina to be seen. The original city of ancient churches and chalk-white houses bleaching in the fierce Sicilian sunlight had been all but swallowed up by the metal and glass towers of the world government—offices, assembly halls, hotels and residence buildings, shops and entertainment centers for the five million men and women who governed the world's twenty-some billions.

In his air-conditioned, soundproofed office atop the tallest of all the towers, the General Chairman could not hear the shrill voices of the crowded streets below, nor the constant growl of cars and turbotrucks on the busy throughways.

At least we saved some of the old city, he thought. It had been one of his first successes in world politics. A small thing. But he had helped to stop the growth of the New Messina before it completely choked and killed the old city. The new city had remained the same size for nearly thirty years now.

Beyond the fishing boats at the city's waterfront, the Straits sparkled invitingly under the sun. And beyond that, the tip of Italy's boot, Calabria, where the peasants still prided themselves on their hard-headed stubbornness. And beyond the misty blue hills of Calabria, shimmering in the heat haze, the sterner blue of the sky was almost too bright to look at.

The old man knew it was impossible, but he thought he saw the glint of one of the big orbital stations hovering in that brilliant sky. He worked a forefinger and thumb against the bridge of his nose. It was one of those days when he felt his years.

He thought about his native São Paulo, how it spread like a festering sore all the way from the river to the sea, flattening hills, carving away the forest, bursting with so many people that not even the Population Control Center's computers could keep track of them. No sane man would willingly enter the heart of São Paulo, or any large city on Earth. No human being could live in the teeming guts of a city and keep his sanity.

How hard they had worked to save the cities! How hard they had worked to make the world safe and stable.

And now this.

The desk top intercom chimed.

"Yes?" The Chairman automatically switched from the Portuguese of his thoughts to the English of the world government.

His secretary sensed his mood. Her face was somber instead of showing its usual cheerfulness. "They're here, sir."

Nodding, "Very well. Send them in."

Six men and two women filed into the spacious office and took seats at the conference table. The women sat together up at the end closest to the windows, next to the head chair. They carried no papers, no briefcases. Each place at the table had a tiny intercom and viewscreen that linked with the central computer.

They are young and vital, thought the Chairman. *They know what must be done and they have the strength to do it. As soon as all this is settled, I shall retire.*

Reluctantly he took his place at the head of the glistening mahogany table. The others remained silent, waiting for him to speak. The only sound was the faintest whir of the computer's recording spool.

He cleared his throat. "Good morning. Last Monday we discussed this situation and you made your recommendation. I asked you to consider possible alternatives. From the looks on your faces, it seems that no suitable alternative has been found."

They all turned to the stocky, round-faced Minister of Security, Vassily Kobryn. He had the look of an athlete to him: tanned skin, short, wiry brown hair, big in the shoulders and arms.

Shifting in his chair self-consciously, Kobryn said, "I see I have been elected the hatchet man." His voice was deep and strong, with barely a trace of a Slavic accent. "All right . . . it *was* my idea, originally. We looked at all the possibilities and ran each case on the computers. The only safe way is to put them in exile. Permanently."

"Siberia," one of the women muttered.

"No, not Siberia." Kobryn took her literally. "It's too heavily populated. Too many cities and dome farms for an effective exile. No, the only place is the new space station. It's large enough and it can be kept completely isolated."

Rolf Bernard, the Minister of Finance, shook his head. "I still disagree. Two thousand of the world's leading scientists . . ."

"Plus their wives and families," the Chairman added.

"What would you prefer?" Kobryn snapped. "A bullet in each of their heads? Or would you leave them alone and let them smash everything that we have worked for?"

"Perhaps if we talked with them . . ."

"That won't work," said Eric Mottern, the taciturn Minister of Technology. "Even if they tried to cooperate with us, you can't stop ideas from leaking out. And once this genetic engineering idea gets loose . . ."

"The world is turned upside down," the Chairman said. He spoke softly, but everyone heard him. With a sigh, he confessed, "I have also been thinking about the problem. I have also tried to find alternatives. There are none. Exile is the only permissible answer."

"Then it is agreed. Good!" said Kobryn.

"No, not good," the General Chairman said. "Very far from good. When we do this thing, we admit failure. We admit fear—yes, terror. We are terrified of a new idea, a new scientific discovery. The government of the world, the protectors of peace and stability, must stoop to exiling some of the world's finest minds. This is a horrible state of affairs. Truly horrible."

Chapter 2

Lou Christopher leaned back in his chair and put his feet up on the desk: his favorite position for thinking. In his lap he held a small tablet and a pen. Although he was both worried and puzzled, his face showed neither of these emotions. He was frowning and looked more angry than anything else.

Through the plastiglass partition that made up one wall of his small office, Lou could see Ramo, the Institute's main computer, flashing its console lights as it worked.

"Come on, Ramo," he muttered to himself, "get it right this time."

Lou tapped the pen on the tablet and watched the little viewscreen on his desk. It was blank. Then . . .

"I'm sorry," Ramo said in a warm baritone voice from the overhead speaker, "but the possible permutations are still three orders of magnitude beyond my programming instructions."

"Three orders!"

"I can proceed with the existing matrix, or await further programming." Ramo's voice sounded neither worried nor puzzled. Not happy nor angry. He was simply stating facts.

Lou tossed the pen back onto the desk and slammed his feet to the floor. The tablet fell off his lap.

"Still three orders of magnitude to go." Lou shook his head, then glanced at his wristwatch. It was already nine A.M.

"I'm waiting for instructions," Ramo said calmly.

You and your instructions can both . . . Lou caught himself, realizing that the computer wasn't at fault. There were millions upon millions of branching pathways in the human genetic code. It was simply going to take more time to get them all programmed properly.

Shrugging, he said, "Okay, Ramo, looks like we've got a full day ahead of us."

Ramo said nothing, but somehow Lou felt that the computer nodded in agreement.

Lou got up and walked out of the office, past the computer's humming, light-blinking main console, out into the hall. He got a cup of water from the cooler, gulped it down as he looked out the hallway window at the New Mexico morning outside. It had been barely dawn when Lou drove to the Institute. Now it was full daylight, bright and cloudless.

Half the gliders have already taken off, Lou thought glumly. *I just won't make this race. Better call Bonnie.*

Tossing the plastic cup into the recycling slot in the wall, Lou went back to his office, plopped tiredly into his cushioned chair, and punched the phone button on the desk top.

"Bonnie Sterne," he said. "She's not at home, you'll have to use her pocket phone."

It took a few seconds, then Bonnie's face appeared on the viewscreen. Behind her, Lou could see people bustling around in a crowded room. *She must be in the Control Center,* Lou thought. Sure enough, he heard the muted thunder of one of the big gliders' takeoff rockets.

"Lou! When are you getting out here? I've asked the judges to postpone your takeoff time, but . . ."

He put up his hands. "Better tell them to scratch me. Can't make it today. Probably not tomorrow, either."

"Oh no." Bonnie looked genuinely heartbroken. She was blonde and had light gray eyes, but the finely-etched bone structure of her face always reminded Lou faintly of an Indian's. Maybe it was the high cheekbones, or the cast of her eyes. Maybe she had some Apache blood in her. Lou had always meant to ask but somehow never did.

"Isn't there any way you can get out of it?" she asked. "Can't some of the other programmers do it?"

Lou shook his head. "You know they can't. I'm just as sorry as you are. I've been working toward this race all year. But Kaufman needs this stuff by Monday. The whole Institute's depending on it."

"I know," Bonnie admitted, biting her lower lip. Lou knew that she was trying to figure some way. . . .

"Listen!" she said, suddenly bright again. "Why don't I come down and work with you? Maybe we can finish the programming in time for taking off tomorrow. . . ."

"Thanks, but there's not much you can do. It looks like I'll have to work all night, at least. So I won't be in much shape for flying tomorrow."

Her expression dimmed once more. "It's just not fair. You have to work all weekend . . . and this is the biggest race of the year."

"I know. But genetics comes before racing," Lou said. "You have a good weekend. See you Monday."

"All right. But it's really unfair."

"Yeah. So long."

"So . . . oh, wait! There was a man out here looking for you. Said he was a Federal marshal."

Lou blinked at her. "A what?"

"A Federal marshal. He wanted to see you."

"What for?"

Bonnie shook her head. "I thought marshals were only something in Western stories."

With a grin, Lou said, "Well, we're out in the West, you know."

"But he said he was from New York."

Shrugging, "Well, if he's looking for me, I'll be right here all day."

"If he comes around again, I'll tell him."

"All right." Suddenly curious, Lou asked, "Did he say what he wanted? Why does he want to see me?"

"I don't know," Bonnie replied.

After Bonnie signed off, Lou plunged back into work, doing intricate mathematics problems with Ramo's help and then programming the results into the computer's memory banks. When he looked at his watch again, it was well past noon. He walked down to the cafeteria and took a sandwich and a steaming cup of coffee from the automatic dispensers. The cafeteria was practically empty: only a few of the weekend clean-up crew at the tables.

The scientific staff's out enjoying the weekend, Lou grumbled to himself. Then, *Well, guess they can't do much until I finish programming Ramo.*

He took the plastic-sealed sandwich and coffee back to his office. As he got there, he saw Greg Belsen standing by the computer's main console, watching the big display viewscreen there as it flashed a series of colored drawings and graphs at eyeblink speed.

"What are you doing in here today?" Lou asked.

Greg turned and grinned at him. "Thought you might be lonesome, old buddy. How's it going?"

Lou jabbed a finger toward the viewscreen. "See for yourself. We're still three orders of magnitude off."

Greg gave a low whistle. "That close?"

"Close? It sounds pretty blinking far to me."

Greg laughed. He had an infectious giggle, like a ten-year-old boy's, that was known throughout the Institute. "You're just sore because there's still more work to do. But if you stop to think of where we were six months ago, when you started this modeling program . . ."

"Yeah, maybe," Lou admitted. "But there's still a long way to go."

They walked back into Lou's office together. Greg Belsen was one of the Institute's bright, aggressive young biochemists. He was just short of six feet tall, slightly bigger than Lou. He was lean and flat-gutted from playing tennis and handball, two of the favorite, socially useful sports. Like Lou, Greg had straight dark hair. But his face was roundish and his eyes brown. Lou had more angular features and blue eyes.

"Is there anything I can do to help out?" Greg asked, taking the extra straight-backed chair in Lou's office. "I know you wanted to get to those glider races today. . . ."

Lou sank into the desk chair. "No, there's nobody around here who can program this stuff into Ramo as fast as I can. And Kaufman wants it for Monday morning."

Nodding, Greg said, "I know."

"Is it really that important?"

Greg smiled at him. "I'm not a geneticist, like Kaufman. But I know this—what you're doing now, this zygote modeling, is a crucial step. Until we have it down cold, there's no hope of genetic engineering in any practical sense. But once you've taught Ramo all the ins and outs of the human genetic code, the way is clear. We can be turning out supermen within a year."

Lou leaned back in his chair. "Yeah . . . that's what Kaufman said."

"You're the crucial man," Greg said. "Everything depends on you . . . and your electronic partner."

Not bad for a kid from a hick college, Lou thought to himself.

"Well," Greg said, getting up, "if there's nothing I can do to help, I can at least get out of your way. Guess I'll go see how Big George's doing."

Lou nodded and started to sort through the papers on his desk.

With a grin, Greg added, "Maybe I'll take Bonnie out to dinner . . . seeing's how you've stood her up."

"Hey! Hands off!"

He laughed. "Relax pal. Relax. I don't go poaching. Got a few girls of my own, hidden under rocks here and there."

"Hmph," said Lou.

"But if you can tear yourself away from Ramo for an hour or so, might be a good idea for you to take Bonnie out for dinner. The kid's worked just as hard as you have to get your glider ready for this race, you know. Be a shame to leave her alone all weekend."

"Yeah," Lou agreed. "Maybe I will."

But as soon as Greg left, Lou went back to work. He didn't think about Bonnie or flying or anything else except matching the myriad possible permutations of the human genetic code and storing the knowledge in Ramo's magnetic core memory. It was late afternoon when he was startled out of his concentration by a hard rap on his office door.

Looking up from his paper-strewn desk, Lou saw the door open and a hard-looking, thick-bodied older man stepped in heavily.

"Louis Christopher, I have a Federal warrant for your arrest."

Chapter 3

With mounting anger, Lou asked a thousand questions as the marshal took him from the Institute in a black, unmarked turbocar. The marshal answered none of them, replying only:

"My orders are to bring you in. You'll find out what it's all about soon enough."

They drove to a small private airfield as the fat red sun dipped toward the desert horizon. A sleek, twin-engined jet was waiting.

"Now wait a minute!" Lou shouted as the car pulled up beside the plane. "I know my rights. You can't . . ."

But the marshal wasn't listening to any arguments. He slid out from behind the steering wheel of the car and gestured impatiently toward the jet. Lou got out of the car and looked around. In the lengthening shadows of late afternoon, the airfield seemed deserted. *There must be somebody in the control tower.* But Lou could see no one around the plane, or the hangars, or the smaller planes lined up neatly on the edge of the taxi apron.

"This is crazy," he said.

The marshal hitched a thumb toward the jet again. Shrugging, Lou walked to the open hatch and climbed in. No one else was aboard the plane. The four plush seats in the passenger compartment were empty. The flight deck was closed off from view. As soon as the marshal locked the main hatch and they were both strapped into their seats, the jet engines whined to life and the plane took off.

They flew so high that the sun climbed well back into the afternoon sky. Lou watched the jet's wings slide back for supersonic flight, and then they arrowed eastward with the red sun casting long shadows on the ground, far below. The marshal seemed to be sleeping, so Lou had nothing to do but watch the country slide beneath the plane. They crossed the Rockies, so far below them that they looked more like wrinkles than real mountains. The Mississippi was a tortured gray snake weaving from horizon to horizon. Still the plane streaked on, fast enough to race the sunset.

The sun was still slightly above the horizon when the plane touched down at JFK jetport. Lou had been there once before and recognized it from the air. But their jet taxied to a far corner of the sprawling field, and stopped in front of a waiting helicopter.

The marshal was awake now, and giving orders again. Lou glared at him, but followed his directions. They went out of the jet, across a few meters of cracked grass-invaded cement, and up into the plastic bubble of the copter. Lou sat down on the back bench, behind the empty pilot's seat. The marshal climbed in heavily and sat beside him, wheezing slightly.

Over the whir of the whizzing rotors and the nasal hum of the electric motor, Lou shouted:

"Just where are you taking me? What's this all about?"

The marshal shook his head, slammed the canopy hatch shut, and reached between the two front seats to punch a button on the control panel. The motor hummed louder and the copter jerked up off the ground.

By the time the helicopter flashed over the skyline of Manhattan, Lou was furious.

"Why won't you tell me anything?" he shouted at the marshal, sitting beside him on the back bench. He was leaning back with his burly arms folded across his chest and his sleepy eyes half closed.

"Listen, kid, the phone woke me up at four this morning. I had to race out to the jetport and fly to Albuquerque. I spent half the day waiting for you at that silly glider race. Then I drove to your apartment, and you didn't show up there. Then I went to your lab. Know what my wife and kids are doing right now? They're sitting home, wondering whether I'm dead or alive and why we're not all out on the picnic we planned. Know how many picnics we can afford, on a marshal's pay? Been planning this one all year—had a spot in the upstate park reserved months ago. Now it's going to waste while I hotfoot all across the country after you. So don't ask questions, understand?"

Then he added, "Besides, I don't know what it's all about. I just got the word to pick you up, that's all."

In a softer voice, Lou said, "Well, look . . . I'm sorry about your picnic. I didn't know. . . . Never had a Federal marshal after me before. But why can't I call anybody? My friends'll be worried about me. My girl . . ."

"I told you, don't ask questions." The marshal closed his eyes altogether.

Lou frowned. He started to ask where they were going, then thought better of it. The copter was circling over the East River now, close to the old United Nations buildings. It started to descend toward a landing pad next to the tall graceful tower of marble and glass. In the last, blood-red light of the dying sun, Lou could see that the buildings were stained by nearly a century of soot and grime. The windows were caked with dirt, the once-beautiful marble was cracked and patched.

Two men were standing down on the landing pad, off to one side, away from the downwash of the rotors. As soon as the copter's wheels touched the blacktop, the cabin hatch popped open.

"Out you go," said the marshal.

Lou jumped out lightly. The marshal reached over and yanked the door shut before Lou could turn around. The copter's motor whined, and off it lifted in a spray of dust and grit. Lou pulled his head down and squeezed his eyes shut. When he opened them again, the copter was speeding down the river.

Sun's down now, Lou thought. *He'll never make it in time for his picnic.*

The two men were walking briskly toward Lou, their shoes scuffing the blacktop. One of them was small and slim, Latin-looking. Probably Puerto Rican. The breeze from the river flicked at his black hair. The other somehow looked like a foreigner. His suit wasn't exactly odd, but it didn't look exactly right, either. He was big, blond, Nordic-looking.

"Please come with us," said the Norseman. And sure enough, he had the flat twang of a Scandinavian accent.

"It is my duty to inform you that we are both armed, and escape is impossible."

"Escape from what?" Lou started to feel exasperated again.

"Please," said the Puerto Rican softly. "It is getting dark. We should not remain outside any longer. This way, please."

Well, they're polite enough, at least.

Inside, the UN building looked a little better. The corridor they walked down was clean, at least. But the carpeting was threadbare and faded with a century's worth of footsteps. They took a spacious elevator car, paneled with peeling wood, up a dozen floors. Then another corridor, and finally into a small room.

"Dr. Kirby!"

Sitting on a sofa at the other side of the little room was Dr. John Kirby of Columbia-Brookhaven University. He was in his mid-fifties—white-haired, nervously thin, pinched face with a bent out-thrust nose that gave him the title "Hawk" behind his back.

"I'm sorry," Kirby said. "I don't seem to recall . . ."

"Louis Christopher," said Lou, as his two escorts shut the door and left him alone with Dr. Kirby. "We met at the Colorado conference last spring, remember?"

Kirby made a vague gesture with his hands. "There are always so many people at these conferences. . . ."

Lou sat on the sofa beside him. "I gave a paper on computer modeling for forecasting genetic adjustments. You had a question from the floor about the accuracy of the forecasts. Afterward we had lunch together."

"Oh yes. The computer fellow. You're not a geneticist." Kirby's eyes still didn't seem to really recognize Lou.

"Do you have any idea of what this is all about?" Lou asked.

Kirby shook his head. He seemed dazed, out of it. Lou looked around the room. It was comfortable enough: a sofa, two deep contour chairs, a bookshelf full of tape spools, a viewscreen set into the wall. No windows, though. Lou got up and went to the door. Locked.

Turning back to Kirby, he saw that the old man's face was sunk in his hands. *Did they drug him?*

"Are you okay?" Lou asked.

"What . . . oh, yes . . . I'm all right. Merely . . . well, frankly, I'm frightened."

"Of what?"

Kirby fluttered his hands again. "I . . . I don't know. I don't know why we're here, or what they want to do with us. That's what frightens me. They won't let me call my wife or even a lawyer. . . ."

Lou paced the room in a few strides. "They grabbed me at the Institute. They wouldn't let me call anybody, either. Nobody knows I'm here." Back to the door he paced. "Why are they doing this? What have we done? What's it all about?"

Abruptly the door opened. The same two men stood in the corridor. "You will come with us, please."

Kirby started to stand up. But Lou said, "No I won't. Not until you tell us what this is all about. You can't arrest us and push us around like this. I want to talk . . ."

The Norseman pulled a needle-thin gun from his tunic.

It was so small that his hand hid all of it except the slim barrel. But the muzzle looked as big as a cannon to Lou, because it was pointed straight at him.

"Please, Mr. Christopher. We have no desire to use force. You are not technically under arrest, therefore you have no need for a lawyer. However, you are wanted for questioning at government headquarters in Messina. It would be best if you cooperate."

"Messina? In Sicily?"

The blond nodded.

"But . . . my family," Kirby said in a shaky voice.

"They have been informed," said the Puerto Rican. "No harm will come if you cooperate with us."

With a shrug, Lou headed into the corridor. The Norseman tucked his gun back inside his tunic. The four of them walked slowly down toward the elevator, their footsteps clicking on the bare plastic floors and echoing off the walls. When they got to the elevator, the Puerto Rican touched the DOWN button and instantly the elevator doors slid open.

This building's empty except for us! Lou realized.

He stepped into the elevator, then whirled, grabbed the Puerto Rican and hurled him into the Norseman. They went down in a tangle of arms and legs, shouting. Lou punched the DOOR CLOSE button and yelled to Kirby:

"Come on!"

Kirby stood frozen, his jaw hanging open, as the doors started to slide shut. The Norseman was still on the floor, but he had pushed the Puerto Rican off and was reaching for his gun. The doors shut. Lou pushed the GROUND button and the elevator started down. He could hear somebody pounding on the metal doors at the floor above.

On the ground floor he tried to retrace his steps back to the corridor landing pad outside. He got lost in the corridors, finally saw an EXIT sign, and banged through the doors. It was full night outside, dark and damp-cool, with the ripe acrid smell of the garbage-choked river a sudden shock to Lou's senses. The city was almost completely dark; only a few lights shone, mostly high up in skyscrapers where people had their own power generators and had barricaded themselves in for the night.

He heard footsteps and flattened himself into the deeper shadows along the wall.

"Shall we turn the lights on?" The Norseman's voice.

"And attract every gang of pack rats on the East Side?" the Puerto Rican answered. "You don't know this city very well. He'll never live out the night alone. Either he'll come begging at our doors inside of an hour, or he'll be dead. No one can get through a night on these streets alone."

"My orders are to bring them to Messina unharmed," said the Norseman.

"You want to search for him? Out there? You'll be killed, too."

They said no more. Lou could sense the Norseman shaking his head, not satisfied, but not willing to risk his own skin against the city streets. Lou heard a door click shut. He slid along the wall carefully and found the door he had come through. It was locked from the inside.

He turned away and looked at the city again with new understanding. He was alone in the city.

And the night had just begun.

Chapter 4

Lou hunkered down on his heels, resting his back against the rough wall, and tried to think. He could bang on the door until they came and got him. Then he'd be safe enough. The Norseman might jab him with a sleeping drug, but probably nothing worse. Then they'd take him to Messina. But why? And where was Bonnie? Had they taken her, too?

And why should he let them pull him around by the nose, Lou asked himself with mounting anger. They had no right to take him here. *Who do they think they're pushing around, a frail old professor like Kirby?*

But—out here alone in the city! Lou remembered his high school days in Maryland, when the best way to show you had guts was to sneak into the city at night. Of course, you always went with your friends, never less than a dozen guys. And now that he thought about it, Lou realized that despite their loud claims of bravery they never went deeper than a few blocks into the out-skirts of Baltimore. Then back to the friendly hills of Hagerstown, as fast as their cars could take them. And still John Milford had been killed on that one trip. Lou remembered tripping over his mutilated body as he ran for his car that night. It still made him shiver.

And this was New York, the heart of it at that! The closest place to civilization and safety was the old JFK jetport, out on Long Island someplace.

If I can get to the jetport in one piece, Lou reasoned, *I can get back to Albuquerque. Maybe Bonnie's waiting for me there.*

But how to get to the jetport?

As he sat there wondering, Lou heard the distant whisper of a turbocar. He paid no attention to it at first, but gradually it grew louder and louder. A car! In the city, at night. *Can I get it to stop for me?*

No doubt of it, the whine of the turbine was much closer, coming this way. Lou got up and walked across the blacktopped courtyard, heading for the sound. Far off to his left he saw a glimmer of light. Moving toward him! He ran to the railing that bordered the courtyard. There was a sunken roadway beyond the railing, and down below Lou could see the lights of the approaching car. The roadbed was patched and rough, but apparently some cars still used it.

Lou leaned over the railing and tried to wave at the speeding turbocar. It roared right past him, making his ears pop with the scream of its engine echoing off the walls of the sunken throughway. A puff of hot, grit-laden, kerosene-smelling air blew into his face.

Maybe if I get down to the road I can get somebody to stop and pick me up.

In the darkness left by the passing car, Lou could barely make out a pedestrian bridge spanning the road, down at the end of the courtyard. He trotted to it. A wire screen fence blocked access to it, but Lou scrambled over it like a kid sneaking into a playground after it had been closed for the night.

He crossed the bridge and found himself on the sidewalk of an empty city street. *There's got to be a stairway down to the road someplace along here*, he told himself. He started walking along the street. In the darkness, he stumbled over a bottle and sent it clattering across the pavement. The noise made the city's silence seem more ominous. Lou got up and went on, keeping his eyes on the roadway. The city seemed deserted. But Lou realized that there were people all around him, by the tens of millions. Most of them were barricaded in for the night, terrified of those who roamed the dark. And the rest . . .

Another car raced by, coming up the other way. Lou didn't bother waving. The driver couldn't see him from down on the road. Besides, Lou was beginning to understand that no driver in his right mind would stop to pick up anybody in the heart of the city. It was enough of a chance to drive through the East Side. If the car should break down or have an accident . . .

Maybe if they see I'm wearing a flight suit, Lou tried to convince himself, *they'd stop for me.*

"Goin' somep'ace?"

The voice was like a knife through him. Lou jerked around, startled. A scrawny kid, dressed in rags, was grinning toothily at him.

"Goin' somep'ace?" he repeated.

"Uh . . . I'm lost. I'm trying to find my way. . . ."

Another voice called out from the darkness across the street, "Whatcha got, Pimple?"

"Buck in a funny suit, sez he's losted."

A trio of kids stepped out of the shadows and crossed to where Lou stood, frozen.

"Funny suit," said the one in the middle, the shortest of them all. None of them came up to Lou's shoulder. They were all wearing rags, barefoot, gaunt, scrawny, with the hard, hungry look of starving old men set into the faces of children.

The one in the middle seemed to be the leader. He eyed Lou carefully, then asked, "Got a pass?"

"What?"

"Yer on Peeler turf. Got a pass t'go through?"

"Well . . . no. . . ."

The leader broke into a cackling laugh. "Humpin' right you ain't! Nobody gets a pass, 'cept from me, and I don't give 'em!" All four of them laughed.

Then the leader asked, "How much skin on ya?"

"I don't understand. . . ."

"Skin, leaves, pages, paper, bread. . . ."

"Oh, you mean money," Lou realized. He shook his head. "Nothing. I don't carry . . ."

Something exploded in the small of his back. Lou sagged down to his knees, pain screaming through him. The leader stepped up in front of him. Lou had to look up now to see into his hard, glittering eyes.

"I . . ."

Smiling, the leader rocked back deliberately and then swung his fist into Lou's mouth. One of the other boys kicked Lou in the chest and he toppled over backward, gasping for breath, his mouth suddenly filled with blood, tiny bright lights flashing in his eyes.

He felt their hands on him, ripping open the zips of his

suit, tearing at the fabric. They rolled him over, face down on the filthy sidewalk. They pulled off his boots.

They were talking among themselves now, muttering and giggling. Lou's mouth felt numb and puffy. His back and ribs flamed with pain when he tried to move, but he forced his breathing back to normal, fought his way back up to a crouching position.

"Honest buck, ain't cha?" the leader said, grinning. "No skin, tol' truth. But boots is somethin' ta howl for. Big fer me, but I'll stuff 'em with paper or somethin'."

Lou stayed in his crouch and rubbed at the fast-caking blood on his chin. The four boys were ranged in a half-circle around him, looking very big now as they stood over him.

"Okay," said the leader. "How we gonna get rid of 'im?"

The kid on Lou's left flicked a knife open and started giggling.

Lou uncoiled and slammed straight into the leader, bowling him over, and raced away. He pounded down the darkened street, rounded a corner, and ran as fast as he could, blindly, away from them. Something sharp bit into one bare foot but Lou kept going, heart pounding, sweat pouring all over him.

"A hunt, a hunt!" he heard someone shouting from behind him.

And then the leader's unmistakable voice, "Peelers! A hunt!"

Other voices shouted up ahead, and from a side street too. Lou pulled up short. There was an alley to his right.

Dead end, most likely. He walked, slowly and quietly now, past the alley and toward the corner of the street up ahead. He could feel himself trembling. The pain was buried now beneath the fear. From down the street he heard the scrabbling sounds of barefooted kids walking swiftly toward him.

"Try that alley," somebody said, half a block behind him in the darkness.

Lou turned the corner and started running again.

He lost track of time. Minutes and hours blurred together. Lou only knew that he was running, hunted like a rare gazelle—or more like a meat animal being chased by a pack of wolves. Whenever he stopped, he heard their voices behind him, off to the side, ahead, out of the shadows, everywhere.

He tried to get into the buildings, but the doors were locked. Many of them were sealed with heavy metal screens. Some were electrified, and Lou picked up a handful of burned fingers before he stopped trying the darkened doorways.

"Hey, head 'im off . . . don' let 'im get across the avenya!"

Lou looked up ahead. There were lights glowing a few blocks up the street. One of the main avenues, still lighted? Lights meant civilization, and civilization meant safety. Lou started running toward the lights.

"Hey, there he goes! Get 'im!"

Feet were pounding behind him, getting closer. From around a corner, two boys appeared, knives in hand. Lou swerved out into the middle of the street. When they raced out to meet him, he cut back again in his best touch-football style. One of the boys slipped trying to reach him, and Lou planted a running kick on the other one's midsection so hard that the kid bounced halfway across the street.

The lights, the lights. He had to get to the lights. They were right behind him. A knife whizzed past his head and clattered on the trash-strewn pavement. Lou's lungs were in flames, his heartbeat a deafening roar in his ears. Something grabbed at his waist. He swung around and backhanded viciously. A little kid, no more than eight or nine, spurted blood from his nose as his head snapped back from Lou's blow. He looked afraid and angry and surprised, all at once. Lou grabbed him by the hair and pulled him off, tossed him into the next teenager coming at him, and then sprinted out into the brightly lit avenue.

"Hold it!" roared the leader. "Stop. Don' cross th' line."

Lou stood in the middle of the broad avenue, chest raw and heaving, ears bursting with the hot drumfire of his pulse, legs shaking with fatigue. The kids of the gang bunched together on the sidewalk.

"Good run, funnyman," said the leader. "Lotsa luck." Then he raised his hand.

Lou saw a knife in that hand, saw the leader snap it forward in a quick throw, saw the knife fly through the air toward him. He jumped back, toward the far side of the street. The knife hit point first on the blacktopped street and stuck there, quivering. Now the other boys were slowly reaching for their knives, getting ready to throw.

Stumbling, nearly unconscious from exertion, Lou

backpedaled and then turned and staggered to the pavement on the other side of the avenue. Back away from the lights, into the shadows of a doorway. The kids merely stood on the opposite sidewalk, laughing and standing there, as if waiting for something to happen.

A pair of hands grabbed Lou's arms. "Whatcha want, pinkey?"

Lou never thought he would do it, but he fainted.

Chapter 5

Lou woke up. He was in a room, on the floor. A single, naked bulb up in the ceiling glared at him. A half-dozen kids were standing around him. Black kids. Another gang.

He pulled himself up slowly to a sitting position. Every part of his body ached horribly.

The only furniture in the room was an antique wooden school desk and chair, battered and carved with hundreds of initials. On the wall behind the desk was some sort of old poster showing a huge lion leaping through a ring of fire. The top of the poster had been ripped away. Lou could make out the words . . . EST SHOW ON EARTH, APRIL 15 TO 29. It didn't make any sense to him.

And then he focused on the black man sitting at the desk. He was immense, the biggest man Lou had ever seen. He must have weighed three hundred pounds or more. And he wasn't fat: just huge, giant muscles on a mountainous frame. He looked completely out of proportion to the rickety desk as he sat squeezed in behind it, looming over it and Lou. The only clothing Lou could see was an open vest. His black skin gleamed in the glare of the overhead lamp. It was hard to tell how old he was; he could have been in his early twenties or ten years older.

He was talking to one of the other boys, ignoring Lou's puzzled stare.

". . . only way's gonna be to give 'im back. Otherwise the peace 'tween us an' the Peelers gonna get busted wide open."

"He's ours," the other boy answered hotly. "They lost 'im an' we got 'im. Makes 'im ours, rights?"

The boys muttered agreement.

"You want the Peelers comin' up here after 'im? Ready to fight the whole pack of 'em? Tonight? 'Sides, he ain't got nothin' on 'im, he ain't *worth* keepin'!"

Lou realized they were talking about him. "Hey, wait a minute. . . ."

"Shuddup, pinkey!" A toe nudged his tender back. Lou winced and closed his mouth.

"Naw, wait," said the giant, looking down at Lou. "Know where you are, white man?"

Lou shook his head.

Smiling from the desk, "You're in the secret headquarters of the Top Cats. I am N'Gai Felix Leo, president of the Top Cats. You may call me Felix, for short." Felix spoke very slowly and carefully, in precise English, for Lou. The way a teacher would speak to a backward child.

"Apparently," he went on, "you stumbled into our turf when the Peelers were chasing you a little while ago. We are now discussing whether we should give you back to the Peelers or deal with you ourselves."

"Deal with me?" Lou echoed.

"Kill ya," snapped a tall, lanky kid.

Felix shook his head and grasped the edges of the desk

in his massive hands. "Zonk, whyn't you keep shut?" he said to the kid who had spoken. Turning back to Lou, "You can't stay here. You can't join our gang, for obvious reasons. If we let you go free, the Peelers would take it as an unfriendly gesture and they might start a war with us."

"Them whitesheets," Zonk muttered.

"My friends don't like to admit it," Felix said, his voice rising ever so slightly, "but we are in no shape for a war against the Peelers. They outnumber us badly, and they can call in half a dozen other gangs as allies."

"An' we c'n get all uptown to come on our side!" Zonk shouted.

"Yeah, an' turn the whole city into a battleground?" Felix countered. "Been enough o' that, you fool. We gotta work out somethin' better . . . least, 'til we're strong enough t'stand up t'the Peelers."

"Look," said Lou, "all I want is to get to the jetport before the police block it off. . . ."

"Police?" Zonk flashed. "Helmet heads? After you?"

"Not the tac brigades . . . Federal marshal . . . and some world government people. . . ."

They all stared at him blankly; none of them had the vaguest idea of what Lou was talking about.

Except for Felix. "Why are they after you?"

Lou shrugged. "They won't tell me."

Zonk laughed. "Since when the helmet heads tell you why they crackin' your skull? They jus' *do* it, tha'sall! You find out later in the hospital . . . if you make it that far!"

"If I don't get to the jetport before dawn, they'll probably be waiting for me when I do arrive," Lou said.

Felix shook his head again. "You're not getting to JFK either before dawn or after it. We can't let you go, the Peelers would get sore at us."

"You're just a kneeler!" Zonk yelled. "A chicken, scared o'them damn Peelers!"

Felix's face went unimaginably hard. His eyes slitted, like a cat's. Slowly, ponderously, he rose from his chair and stepped out from behind the desk on legs the size of tree trunks. Zonk glanced around at the other boys, then backed away a step.

"We been friends," Felix said as he advanced like a tide, engulfing the room. His voice was low, menacing. "So I'm gonna give you one chance t'take back that mouth. *Now!*"

"I . . . I . . . I'm sorry," Zonk stammered. "I got sore. . . ."

"Am I a kneeler?" Felix was towering over the skinny boy, scarcely a centimeter away from him. He seemed to surround Zonk.

"No . . . no, you ain't."

"Am I afraid of anything or anyone on this Earth?"

"No. Nothin' or nobody."

Before he could even think of what he was saying, Lou heard his own voice call out, "Then you're not afraid of helping me get to JFK."

Everybody froze. The room went absolutely silent. No one even breathed, it seemed to Lou. Least of all Lou himself. He sat there on the floor, the other boys ranged around him staring open-mouthed, with Felix off to one side, back turned as he confronted the petrified Zonk.

Very, very slowly, Felix turned toward Lou. The grimy

floorboards squeaked under him. His face was still as flat and hard as the face on the lion in the poster.

"What did you say?"

I'm dead either way, Lou told himself. Aloud, he answered, "If you're not afraid of anything or anybody, then you're not afraid of helping me get to the jetport. Tonight. Now."

Felix stared at Lou for a long moment, grim, unblinking. Then slowly his mouth opened and he began chuckling. The chuckle deepened into a laugh, a strong laugh that shook the room. The other kids started laughing, too.

"You're something, white man . . . really something, calling me out like that." Felix roared laughter and went back toward the desk. "You got guts . . . not much brains, maybe, but plenty guts." He dropped back on the chair so hard that Lou felt sure it would crack under him.

Felix shook his head, still laughing. "So you're trying to *dare* me into helping you. That's a jolt, a real jolt."

Lou got to his feet. "Okay, so it's funny. Either help me or kill me or let me go. Take your pick."

Waving a heavy hand, Felix said, "Man, you must have some black blood in you someplace. You got guts, all right. Look . . . if I let you go, you'll get killed before daybreak, y'know? If I help you, it'll start a war. But . . . shoot, baby, it's going to be hard to kill you when you got the guts to dare me."

He turned to Zonk. "Go get us a car."

"You gonna . . ."

"Man wants t'see JFK," Felix said to them. "I ain't seen th' place myself for years. You ever see it?"

Zonk, wide-eyed, shook his head.

"You ready to fight a war when we get back?"

Zonk nodded. So did the others.

"Okay . . . get a car. Maybe we'll stop uptown on our way back, bring down some reinforcements. Show th' Peelers they gotta think twice 'fore they start a war."

"Now you're talkin'," Zonk said, and he headed for the door.

The car was an ancient two-door, crumbling with rust, dented, upholstery ripped, automatic guidance long wrecked, lights defective, radio gone. But it ran. It shook and rattled and whined, but it ran.

They were sputtering down the throughway, air shrilling through ill-fitting windows. Zonk was curled up on the back seat, sleeping. Lou wanted to doze off, too. He ached from his scalp to his bare feet. One foot was throbbing from a cut he had picked up somewhere. But he couldn't sleep. His insides were still as taut as a scream of terror.

They had gone across a bridge, and now the throughway was elevated. The horizon in front of them was just starting to turn gray. The buildings here seemed to be lower and not as closely bunched as back in Manhattan.

Felix was jammed in behind the wheel. He laughed softly. "Man, some people sure are lucky. You got guts all right, but better than that, you got luck."

Lou looked at him. Somehow, in this flat, cold gray of early morning, Felix seemed different.

"Still haven't figured it out, have you?" Felix asked him.

"I don't understand. . . ."

He squirmed around in the too-small bucket seat and glanced over his shoulder at Zonk, who was still sound asleep.

Then he said to Lou, "You think you just talked your way out of being killed by a teen pack? Just like that?" He laughed.

Chapter 6

Lou stared at Felix, who merely chuckled to himself and said no more. Then the towers and hangars of JFK became visible in the predawn glow. Felix pulled the car off the highway and onto an access road.

"What's the matter?" Lou asked.

"Better get ourselves prettied up if we expect to get past the gates at the jetport."

They pulled into the parking lot of an automated, all-night shopping center. Felix woke up Zonk and the three of them walked to the shoppers' mall. Lou's foot was throbbing painfully.

The mall doors were locked, but there was a tiny security unit set into the wall beside them. Lou told his credit number to the receiver grille and let the camera photograph him.

"This credit number is from Albuquerque, New Mexico," said the shopping center computer, impassively. "It will require several moments to check it."

Felix said, "We'll wait."

"If the police are really looking for me," Lou worried out loud, "they'll have my credit number and picture pulled from the file and . . ."

"Sorry to keep you waiting," the computer said without

a trace of regret. "Your credit check is complete. You may enter and purchase whatever you wish, up to a limit of ten thousand dollars."

Felix beamed. "Just what I've always wanted . . . a friend with a good credit rating."

The mall and shops were deserted. Felix waved Zonk off to a men's clothing store and, with his hand firmly on Lou's arm, headed for a drugstore.

"You're really limping. Need that foot taken care of."

"Back in the car," Lou said as they walked through the open doorway of the drugstore, "what'd you mean . . . about me talking my way out of being killed?"

Felix laughed again. "Oh that. Well . . . you're lucky, but not the way you think. Never wonder why the Top Cats are being led by a guy my age? I'm over thirty, you know."

"What are you talking about?"

"Sit down here," Felix said, "while I get some stuff for that foot."

Lou sat in the plastic chair and found himself facing a dispenser-wall of medical supplies. Felix walked slowly down the wall, finding what he wanted in the display windows and touching the buttons that sent the goods down into the receiving bin. He came back to Lou's chair with his hands full of antibiotic sprays and plastic spray bandages.

"Listen," he said as he squirted a disinfectant over Lou's blood-crusted foot, "I'm a teacher. Work for the Office of Rehabilitation. Trying to hammer some sense into these kids. Only way to do it is to join them, lead them, try to bring them around slowly. I been in there, in the city, for more than a year now. Got them to set up boundaries between turfs. Trying to get them to think of more than sex and wars. I figure it'll take another ten to twelve years before they start acting as civilized as Stone Age tribes."

"They don't know . . ."

Felix laughed. "Shoot, man, if they knew, I'd be just as dead as you ought to be!" Then his face went grim. "Some of the other teachers have been found out. What happened to them isn't pretty."

"But why do you do it?"

Shrugging, "How should I know? Can't just leave the kids in there by themselves. Too many generations have done that. Every year they get worse off and worse off until they're where they are now. *Somebody's* got to help them. We owe them something. They didn't turn into savages by themselves. They were pushed. And unless somebody starts pushing from the other direction, those kids are going to keep on killing, keep on dying."

Lou said, "It'll take a hundred years before kids like that become civilized."

"So we'll work a hundred years," Felix snapped. "Took more than a hundred years to let the cities fall apart like this. It's worth a century to rebuild them. Because if we don't—if we let those kids keep breeding and festering like they've been for the past century—pretty soon they're going to burst out of the cities and overrun everything. The Mongol hordes will seem like a Chinese tea party compared to what they'll do."

Lou shuddered.

"But it's more than that," Felix went on. "Those kids deserve a chance. They never asked to be born into that jungle. They never got a chance for anything better. And they'll never know anything better unless some of us get off our rumps and try to help 'em. Those kids are the future, y'know. What good's all our high and mighty civilization if we lose those kids? What use is all this technology and science if we're breeding cavemen in the cores of the cities? If we can't help those kids make their own future better, we don't have much to look forward to, I can tell you that."

"You ought to be a Congressman, or a minister," Lou said.

Felix laughed.

"And all that talk about killing me. . . ."

"Oh, that was real all right," he said. "I was trying to figure out some way to get your white hide out of there. But I wasn't coming up with any answers. Looked like I was going to let them take you out. . . ."

"You'd've let them?"

Another shrug. "Couldn't figure out what else to do, until you started talking tough. Gave me the out I needed."

"Well . . . thanks, I guess."

"Don't mention it," Felix replied, grinning.

Within half an hour, Lou was walking with hardly a limp. He showered, shaved, and put on a disposable summer suit and loafers that he picked out at the clothing store. Felix and Zonk had outfitted themselves, too. Felix went in for grander tastes, complete with cape and boots.

Zonk leaned toward electric colors and the latest, form-fitted, sprayed-on styles.

"You look almost decent," Felix said to Lou. "Mouth's still swollen and you've got a nice blue lump coming along over your eye. But you'll be okay."

Felix drove them through the main gates of JFK just as the sun showed itself over the distant skyline. The white-helmeted security guards at the gates eyed the battered old car, but let it pass. Up the sweeping ramp of the once-grand terminal building they went, with Felix steering carefully to avoid potholes.

He stopped in front of the terminal and Lou got out, then ducked his head back in and put his hand in Felix's huge paw. "Thanks. For everything. And good luck."

"Nothing to it," Felix said, grinning. "Hope you make out okay." Then he turned to Zonk and said, "C'mon up front. Le'see what jet planes look like up close."

The clattering car drove off. Lou stood there for a moment in the growing light of dawn watching them disappear down the other side of the ramp. Then he turned and went inside the decaying terminal.

The first flight that connected with Albuquerque wasn't until seven. An hour to wait. His insides fluttering from hunger as much as nerves, Lou went to the autocafeteria and had powdered eggs, reconstituted milk, and a man-made slice of something called protosteak. It tasted like plastic.

No one stopped him or even noticed him as he went to the flight departure lounge, verified his ticket on the jet, went aboard, and took his seat. The plane was ten minutes late getting away from the terminal, and Lou expected each second to see the same Federal marshal come up the aisle and clap a hand on his shoulder.

But finally they were airborne. As soon as Lou heard the wheels pull up, he fell asleep.

He woke up with a start when the flaps and wheels went down again. Out the window he could see the familiar flat greenery of the New Mexico irrigated farmlands. Off in the distance, Sandia Peak stuck its rocky brown mass up into the sky.

I wonder if Bonnie's home. Maybe she never left for Charleston. Then another thought hit him. *What if they're waiting for me when I get off the plane?*

The plane landed and taxied up to the terminal. Lou put himself in the middle of the ninety-some people who were getting off and tried to look invisible in the crowd. He stayed in the crowd until he was well into the terminal, then headed straight for the exit, looking over his shoulder a few times to see if anyone was following him. No one. Outside in the blazing sunlight, he wondered if his car was still in the parking lot. *Better leave it alone.* He waved for a cab, and one pulled away from its parking stall and glided to the curb where he stood.

Inside, after he firmly shut the cab door, Lou told the autodriver, "Genetics Institute."

If Bonnie wasn't picked up by the police, she'll be at the lab. And Dr. Kaufman and the others . . . they'll help me.

The cab drove out away from the city, into the farm-lands, along one of the main irrigation lines. For the thousandth time, Lou tried to puzzle out why the police wanted him. The Federal marshal said he was under arrest. The Norseman at the UN building said he wasn't. But they were going to take him to Messina. Why? *Better check with Greg at the Institute and see if he knows a good lawyer.*

Finally, Lou could see the familiar white buildings of the Institute. Almost immediately, he could tell that something was wrong.

The place looked deserted. The parking lot was empty. Nobody was walking around outside. Nobody was visible in the big glass-fronted lobby. And as the cab pulled up to the outer fence, the gate did not slide open automatically.

Lou looked at his wristwatch. It was still on Albuquerque time; he hadn't changed it. It said nine-thirty.

Why is it . . . wait a minute! What day is it? Sunday or Monday? I took off . . . it must be Sunday, got to be.

He thumbed the window button down and felt the heat of the outdoors invade the cab. To the gate control box he said, "Code one-five, Christopher. Open up."

The gate rattled open. The cab drove smoothly up to the lobby door. Just to be safe, Lou gave a phony name and credit number to the cab's simple-minded computer. It had no camera equipment and therefore no way to check on who its passenger really was.

As the cab drove away, Lou stood squinting in the brilliant sunshine. For a moment, a flash of fear knifed through him. Even for a Sunday the Institute seemed utterly deserted. Usually there was *somebody* around.

"Well," he said to himself in a deliberately loud, firm voice, "I can hide out here until some of the staff shows up tomorrow. Or maybe I'll call Greg or one of the other guys. . . ."

The main doors into the lobby were locked also, but Lou's name and code symbol were enough to open them. He stepped into the quiet, cool darkness of the lobby; the sun's glare was screened out by the polarized windows. He hesitated a moment, then walked through the open doorway and into the building's main corridor. His footsteps against the plastic flooring and the whisper of the air conditioning were the only sounds he could hear.

First thing to do is call Bonnie, he thought, *find out if she's okay.*

His own office was down at the end of the corridor, next to Ramo, the big computer. Suddenly Lou realized, *Not even Ramo's making any noise!* Usually, the computer was humming and chattering electronically; it was almost always working on something, even on weekends and late at night.

Lou looked through the glass partition that surrounded Ramo. The computer was silent. No lights flashing on its main board.

"Ramo, you awake?" Lou called.

From a speaker in the ceiling overhead came Ramo's baritone voice. "Yes, Lou. I'm fine. What can I do for you?" A single row of lights on the main board flickered to life.

Lou breathed a relieved sigh. "You were so quiet. . . . I thought somebody had shut you down."

"All programs are completed at present," Ramo answered.

"All programs? What about the zygote modeling calculations?"

"That program was temporarily shut down by Dr.
Kaufman."

"Shut down? Why?"

"I don't know."

Lou stood there watching the flickering row of lights,
uncertain, feeling something like panic forming in the pit
of his stomach. He fought it down. "Okay . . . uh, get
Bonnie Sterne on the phone for me, will you? Her home
phone."

"Shall I place the call on your office phone?" Ramo
asked.

"No . . . I'll be in the cafeteria. Anybody been in
today?"

"No one. Except for Big George, of course."

Shaking his head in puzzlement, Lou went back up the
corridor and turned down a side hall to the cafeteria. His
head was throbbing with pain, and despite his nap on the
plane he felt dead tired. And hungry.

Lou was surprised to see Big George sitting in the cafeteria, eating a huge plate of fruit salad.

Big George was an eight-year-old mountain gorilla,
taller than Lou, even in his hunched-over, ground-knuck-
ling posture. No one had weighed him for several
months, since he playfully ripped the big scales they had
used out of the wall of his special quarters. His face was
all ferocity—fanged mouth, low beetling brow, black
muzzle, and blacker hair. His arms could reach across the
table without his ever getting up from the chair he was

sitting on. The plastic chair itself was sagging dangerously under his weight. It was hard to believe that Big
George was a gentle, even a timid, animal.

"Who let you in here?" Lou asked from the doorway.

"Let myself in, Uncle Lou," George whispered. "Got
hungry. Nobody here to feed me. Opened the pen gate
and came in for food."

Lou went over to the selector wall and punched buttons for a real steak dinner. "You mean nobody's been
around to feed you since yesterday?"

"Nobody, Uncle Lou." George stuffed half a cantaloupe
into his toothy mouth. Big George was one of the Institute's great successes. The geneticists had managed to
give the gorilla a large measure of intelligence. George
tested out to the intelligence level of a human six-year-
old. It seemed that he would not go any further. The
surgical team that worked with the Institute had altered
George's vocal equipment so that he could speak in a
harsh, labored whisper. It was the best they could do.

Lou carried his steaming tray to the end of the table
where George was sitting. He was glad of some compan-
ionship, but it was best to give George plenty of room.
Not that he was dangerous—just sloppy.

Looking up at the ceiling, Lou called, "Hey, where's
that phone call, Ramo?"

"There is no answer," came the smooth reply.

"She's not home?"

"Evidently not," said Ramo.

"What's her phone say?"

"Nothing. No reply whatsoever. No forwarding number, no request to leave a message."

Lou stared down at his steak. Suddenly he wasn't hungry anymore.

"Ramo!" he shouted. "Where is everybody?"

"All of the scientific staff has been taken into custody by Federal marshals," Ramo said calmly. "Everyone else has been sent home."

Before it could really register on Lou's mind, George growled, "Somebody coming in the hallway, Uncle Lou. Strangers."

"Federal marshals," Ramo said. "I was programmed to call them when you returned to the Institute."

Chapter 7

Lou stood up, hot fear burning through him. "Federal marshals?"

"They have locked all the doors and are searching the building for you," Ramo said without emotion.

"Uncle Lou, I'm afraid," George whispered.

"How many of them are there?" Lou asked Ramo.

"Twelve."

Big George pushed off his chair and shambled over to stand beside Lou, so close that Lou could feel the warmth from his great hairy body. George was terrified. *But the marshals don't know how timid he really is. They might shoot as soon as they see him.*

"Is the door to the courtyard locked?"

"Yes," Ramo answered. "All the doors are."

There were footsteps in the hall now; Lou could hear them. He turned to George, snuffling fearfully beside him.

"Can you knock that door open, Georgy?"

"I can try, Uncle Lou."

Lou patted his massive shoulder. "Come on, quick."

George scampered toward the door, accidentally knocking a chair clattering out of his way. From out in the hall a voice called:

"Hey . . . hear that? In here, quick, unlock it!"

George was loping across the floor in full stride now, knuckles and big splayed feet slapping the tiles. Lou had to run to keep up with him. George didn't stop or even slow down at the door. He simply crashed right through, his bulk and speed tearing the lock right apart and knocking both doors off their hinges with a blood-freezing shriek of ripping metal.

Lou was right behind him in the sudden glare of the sunshine.

"George . . . this way!"

Now Lou took the lead, through the courtyard and out the access tunnel toward the back lot. Stopping, he pointed to the stand of trees off behind the parking area.

"You . . . get back . . . to your pen," he panted. "Safest place . . . for you. They won't bother you . . . in there."

"But Uncle Lou, I want to go with you," George argued hoarsely. "All the nice people went away. These new people scare me."

Lou took a deep breath and said, "They won't hurt you. And you can't come with me right now. But I'll come back for you."

"When?"

Lou could hear shouts out in the courtyard.

"As soon as I can, Georgy."

"Promise?"

"I promise. Now get back to your pen and be a good boy. And don't be afraid, they won't hurt you."

With a troubled look, the gorilla moved off toward the trees.

Lou sprinted for the parked cars. The lab's electric wagons were lined up in the first row, and Lou knew their ignition locks were keyed to a simple voice code. He slid in behind the wheel of the first one in line.

"DNA–RNA," he said as he pressed the starter switch.

The electric motor hummed to life. *Never be able to outrun turbocars in this thing,* Lou told himself. A man in a gray business suit ran out onto the parking lot. He had a gun in his hand. Lou grabbed the steering wheel, kicked off the brakes, and slammed the accelerator to the floor. The wagon lurched feebly, then started to gain momentum. Lou drove straight at the man. He jumped away and fired. Lou swung the wagon away and then cut back for the access tunnel, dived through its shadow, raced through the courtyard and past another handful of jumping, shouting men, into the front tunnel and out past the main lobby.

The front gate was rolling shut, but Lou knifed the wagon through it and sped down the highway in the curiously quiet acceleration of the electric motor. He picked up the car radio microphone and called:

"Ramo, this is Lou Christopher. Over."

"I recognize your voice pattern, Lou. Over."

"Basic program zero, Ramo. Suspend all housekeeping functions until further notice. Maintenance and repair mode only. Execute. Over."

"Executed. Over."

Lou grinned as he raced down the highway, one hand on the wheel. "Very good, Ramo. Now suspend all communications until my voice pattern orders resumption. Understood? Over."

"Understood and prepared to execute," Ramo said tonelessly. But somehow Lou felt the computer didn't like to shut itself off.

"Execute. Over."

No answer. The computer was completely shut down. All the doors that were locked would remain locked until some of the Institute maintenance men could be brought in to open them manually. The front gate would stay locked too, and it was strong enough to keep the police cars inside even if they tried ramming it. All the lights, the air conditioning, everything, was off. *Have a pleasant day!* Lou thought grimly.

He eased off the accelerator and coasted down the highway at the legal maximum speed. No sense getting picked up by a traffic patrol. His insides were fluttering, now that he had enough time to think.

How long can I keep running? Where to now? Not my apartment. Ramo said everybody on the scientific staff was arrested. Did they take Bonnie, too? And why, why, for God's sake? What's going on?

He shook his head. It was like a nightmare. It couldn't be real. Police don't just march into a lab and arrest everybody. That was something out of the Dark Ages. People have rights, there are laws. . . .

And then he remembered New York, and realized that in some places the Dark Ages still existed.

As he drove toward town, Lou switched on the radio and dialed to the police frequency. Plenty of chatter, but nothing about the Institute or himself. *Why not? Why aren't they calling for help? Or at least spreading an alert to pick me up?*

As if in answer, Lou saw a highway patrol cruiser gliding up behind him on the outside lane. He knew that the electric wagon could never outspeed a cruiser; the turbine-driven police car could even lift itself off the ground and literally fly on an air cushion for short distances, doing several hundred knots. But the cruiser zipped right past him, and the two white-helmeted officers in it never even looked at him.

Maybe the police aren't after me, Lou said to himself.

Another part of his mind answered, *Somebody is.*

But not the police. Then who are they?

A few minutes later he found himself driving past Bonnie's apartment building. *Got to stop someplace. Got to have some time to figure this out. Even if she's been picked up, I can still use her apartment. And if she's free, I can find out what's going on from her.*

He drove the wagon halfway across town, parked it in a public garage, and then took a cab back to Bonnie's. He gave the cab another false name and credit number. In the lobby of the apartment building, he told the door-computer:

"I'm a friend of Miss Sterne's, apartment 27-T."

"Name, please," the computer's flat voice replied.

"Roy Kendall," Lou lied, naming a mutual friend who lived in Denver.

"Miss Sterne is not in at present. I am not programmed to admit anyone."

"Miss Sterne has left special instructions under Code V for visitors."

The computer hummed to itself for a second. Then,

"Mr. Kendall, you may be admitted." The door clicked open. Lou stepped through and went to the elevator.

He had to go through the same routine with the lock computer at Bonnie's door, but here the code symbol was sf for special friends. Finally, the door popped open and Lou stepped into Bonnie's apartment.

Shutting the door carefully behind him, Lou looked over the single room. Nothing seemed disturbed or moved. The closet next to the foldaway bed was open, and there were some clothes draped on a chair in front of it. Lou poked into the kitchenette alcove and found a pot of coffee still plugged in and warm. *Bonnie was here this morning. Or at least, somebody was here.*

He took a bottle of milk from the refrigerator and downed half of it. He was just putting it back when the front door opened.

Bonnie stood in the doorway, open-mouthed with surprise.

"Lou!"

She ran to him and threw herself into his arms. She felt warm and soft and safe.

"Baby, is it ever good to see you," he murmured into her ear as he held her. "You even *smell* great."

"Lou, what happened to you? Where've you been? We heard . . . Oh, Lou, your face!" She reached up and touched his swollen jaw. It hurt, but Lou didn't mind at all.

"It's a long story," he said, still holding her tightly. "For a while there, I didn't think I'd ever see you again."

He kissed her, and then she gently pulled away. For

the first time, Lou noticed she looked tired, strained.

"What's been going on?" he asked. "Why's the Institute been closed? Ramo said . . ."

"You've been at the Institute?" She looked startled.

Lou nodded. "Yep. Nearly got caught by a squad of guys who claimed to be Federal marshals."

"They *were* marshals," Bonnie said.

"But what's this all about?"

Bonnie went toward the sofa, by the windows on the other side of the room. Lou followed her there.

Sitting, she told him, "The first I heard about it was yesterday, at the glider races. There was a Federal marshal looking for you. Then, when I got back to my apartment, there was another marshal waiting for me. I had to go with him to the Federal courthouse. Practically everybody in the Institute was there!"

Lou sank back in the sofa, realizing now why Bonnie looked strained.

"They let some of us out after a few hours," she went on, her voice trembling a little. "But we were told not to go back to the Institute anymore. It's been closed down."

"Closed?"

Nodding, "Permanently, they said. I had to report to the employment center this morning. That's where I've been all day. Lou . . . what are they doing?" Her voice was starting to rise now, her tiny fists were clenched. "Why did they close the Institute? What is it? What?"

He took her by the shoulders. "Hey . . . ease off now," he said softly. "Take it easy. You're okay. Nobody's going to hurt you."

"But they brought in Dr. Kaufman, and Greg Belsen, and just about all the scientists. All the technicians, all the secretaries and clerks . . . everybody!"

"But why? Did they give you any reason?"

She shook her head. "Nothing. Nobody seemed to know anything. They were just following orders." She reached out and touched his jaw again. "But what happened to you?"

"I got away." Lou told her about his night in New York, and this morning's visit to the deserted Institute.

"What are you going to do now?" Bonnie asked.

"I don't know," he admitted. "I'm about ready to cave in. Only had a couple hours' sleep on the jet. . . ."

Bonnie stood up. Brushing a blonde lock from her eyes, she said, "I'll fix you some lunch and then you can take a nap."

She went to the kitchenette alcove and started touching buttons on the control keyboard. Lou slouched on the sofa, already half asleep.

"Lou . . . it's like the world's coming apart, isn't it?"

He looked up at her. "Whatever it is, it's bigger than the Institute. They had Kirby from Columbia at the UN building. They were going to take us to Messina. . . ."

"The world capital?"

Lou nodded. "I guess the world government's behind this. And they've got the Federal people here on their side. But why? What's it all about?"

Bonnie took a pair of steaming trays from the cooker and placed them on the low table next to the sofa. She sat on the floor, next to Lou's feet.

"Lou . . . if the world government is after you—then there's no place for you to hide!"

"Maybe," he muttered, leaning over the trays and picking up a fork.

Bonnie said, very softly, "Maybe the only thing you can do is give yourself up. After all, if it's the world government, it must be something terribly important, whatever it is."

"But what are they up to?" Lou demanded. "Why yank us in like we're criminals? Why haven't they told us what's going on? They haven't called in the local police. And they're sure not giving us any chances to exercise our constitutional rights."

Bonnie didn't answer.

They ate in silence, and then Lou stretched out on the sofa for a nap. He dreamed of being chased through the streets of New York by gangs of kids and uniformed policemen. Somehow the streets became Messina, but the gangs still pursued him. And from a balcony above him, Felix leaned heavily on a frail railing, huge and black, booming laughter at the chase.

He woke up shouting. Bonnie was beside him, her hands on him, stroking him. He sat up.

"They . . . I . . ."

"It's all right," she said soothingly, "it's all right. You were dreaming. Look, you're in a cold sweat."

Lou ran a hand over his eyes.

"Bonnie . . ."

She looked away from him and said, "Lou, while you were sleeping, I was thinking hard about this whole thing. You can't run away forever. You were lucky to get away last night without being killed. Sooner or later, they'll either catch you or you'll get hurt or killed."

"Yeah, I guess so. But what else . . ."

Bonnie's hands were clenched together in white-knuckled tenseness. Her face looked bleak.

"Lou," she said, "I don't want you to get hurt. I . . . while you were asleep I called the courthouse. There are four marshals outside in the hall. They've come for you."

"You *what!*" Lou sprang up from the sofa.

"There's no other way out of here," she said. There were tears in her eyes now as she stood beside him. "Please, Lou . . . let them take you in. They promised that nobody's going to hurt you. Please . . ."

Lou stared at her. "Federal marshals, the world government, the Institute closed . . . and now even you, even you, Bonnie. Nobody in the world is on my side. Nobody! In the whole world!"

"Lou, please . . ." She was crying now.

The door opened and they walked in. Four of them. Big-shouldered, tight-lipped. Wearing plain, dark business shorts and tunics. Armed, everybody knew, with needle guns and more.

"Louis Christopher. I have a Federal warrant for your arrest."

"Nobody in the whole stupid world," Lou muttered loudly enough for only Bonnie to hear.

Chapter 8

In a way, Lou felt almost glad that his running was over. It was like the time he had an inflamed appendix, but didn't know it. For weeks he nursed the sullen pain in his abdomen, worried over it, but told no one. Until he nearly collapsed at the Institute and some of the other computer engineers physically dragged him to the clinic. From then on he didn't have to make any decisions. And he found that he didn't worry, either. The doctors did the deciding, and the worrying.

Now Lou sat in the back of a car, surrounded by Federal marshals. All the decisions were out of his hands. He stopped worrying, almost without realizing it. He was far from being happy, but for the time being he had nothing to worry over.

They drove to the jetport, past the terminal building, out to a sleek, white, twin-engine executive jet parked well away from all the hangars and commercial planes. The sky-blue insignia of the world government was painted on its tail.

Standing beside the plane, next to the open hatch, was the Norseman Lou had narrowly escaped from at the UN building.

He looked Lou over carefully as the Federal marshals escorted him to the plane.

"I see you made it through New York and then some," said the Norseman. "Congratulations. We were afraid you'd be killed."

Lou said nothing.

"Please, Mr. Christopher, my job is to bring you safely to Messina. No more adventures, eh? We'll only have to come and get you again."

He gestured toward the hatch. With a shrug, Lou climbed into the plane. The Norseman followed him and locked the hatch shut, then went forward, into the control compartment. The jet was luxuriously furnished with big, deep swivel seats at the four forward windows. Back of them there was a couch on one side, and a full-sized desk on the other, complete with viewphones.

The Norseman re-emerged from the control compartment. "Pick any chair you like. This flight is exclusively for you."

Within minutes they were airborne and streaking supersonically across the country. They landed briefly at New Washington for fuel, then headed out across the Atlantic with the setting sun at their back. Lou slept as the plane sped into the gathering night.

The Norseman woke him when they were ready to land. It was black and moonless outside, and the only lights Lou could see below outlined a landing strip. Once on the ground, Lou was taken to a waiting car and driven away from the airfield. The Norseman sat silently beside him while two swarthy men spoke Italian to each other up in the front seat. All Lou could see was the narrow strip of road lit by the car's headlights, but he got the impression of hills and farmlands and wind-tossed trees swaying out there in the darkness. It was warm outside, and the night had that special softness that comes from the sea, very different from the desert of New Mexico.

Before long they drove past a gateway that was flanked by two live guards. After a few minutes more, the car pulled onto a driveway that swung up to an ornately decorated entrance, lit by antique lanterns. It even had an awning overhead to keep off the sun and rain. It was hard to tell how big the building was, but in the darkness it gave the impression of rambling on hugely. *A villa*, Lou guessed as the car stopped in front of the entrance.

The Norseman got out first and held the car door open as Lou slid along the seat and stepped out. From far off he could hear the sighing roar of the sea rolling in on a beach.

"This will be your home for the time being," the Norseman said, pointing to the baroquely carved door. "I believe you'll find many of your friends there."

He stood there while Lou slowly, hesitantly, went up the stone walkway and tried the door. It opened at his touch. Lou looked back and saw the Norseman smiling and nodding at him.

"Your job's done now, is that it?"

"Yes," he answered. "You were the last one on the list."

What list? Lou wanted to ask, but he knew that he wouldn't get an answer. He stepped into the entryway of the villa and the door swung shut by itself behind him. Lou knew somehow that it locked automatically. He didn't bother to try it.

He stood alone in a wide, long hall. At the far end a grand flight of stairs swept in a gentle curve to the next floor. There were heavy doors of real wood on both sides of the hall, and the walls were lined with paintings. Portraits, mostly. Old and original. A stately grandfather's clock back by the stairs chimed once. One A.M.

Lou walked down the hall slowly, his footsteps echoing on the intricate geometry of the parqueted floor. No other sound—no, wait. Voices, muted, from behind a door. He went over and opened it.

A half-dozen men were sitting around a table in the middle of the room. It must have been a library or study; books lined the walls except for a pair of French doors that stood open at the far end of the room. Their filmy curtains billowed softly in the breeze coming in off the sea. The room was dimly lit and most of the men at the table had their backs to the door and to Lou. One of them looked up.

"Lou! They dragged you in finally."

It was Greg Belsen.

Now the others turned to face him. They were all from the Institute: Ron Kurtz, Charles Sutherland, Jesse Maggio, Bob Richardson. And at the head of the table, Dr. Adrian Kaufman, Director of the Institute. Dr. Kaufman was a handsome, vigorous man, with strong leonine features topped by thick gray hair. But right now he looked very weary and unsure of himself.

"Christopher," said Dr. Kaufman, frowning slightly. "What on earth are you doing here?"

Despite himself, Lou grinned, "It wasn't my idea to come, believe me."

Lou walked to the table. There were no more chairs in the room, so he remained standing.

"Why did they bring you here?" Dr. Kurtz asked. He was about Lou's age, but his bushy brown beard made him look older. "So far the only people here are the scientists."

By *scientists*, Lou understood, Kurtz meant geneticists and biochemists.

"That's right," Dr. Maggio agreed. "Only the technical staff has been brought here. They let the secretaries and others go free."

"I am on the technical staff," Lou reminded them.

"But as a computer engineer, not a geneticist," said Dr. Kurtz.

"Or biochemist," added Dr. Richardson, a biochemist.

"Maybe the people who arrested us don't know the difference between computer engineers and geneticists," Lou said, feeling anger simmering inside him. "Maybe they just had orders to bring in the whole technical staff. They sure didn't stop and ask to see my diploma."

"Well," Greg Belsen said, "there goes the neighborhood. If they start letting computer people in, God knows what'll happen next."

The scientists all laughed. Lou realized that Greg was trying to smooth over the rift between the scientists and himself. It was an old wound, this caste system. Under ordinary circumstances at the Institute it hardly ever became noticeable. But here, in this strange place, it surfaced immediately. And it hurt.

Dr. Richardson changed the subject. "Does anyone have any idea of why we're here?"

"You used the word 'arrested,'" Dr. Kaufman said to Lou. "As far as I know, no one has arrested us. We've been brought here against our will, true enough. But no one has charged us with a crime."

"More like being kidnapped."

"I was arrested by Federal marshals," Lou said. "No charges, but they were ready to shoot if I tried to get away. And the Institute's been closed permanently, I found out."

"*Permanently!*" The word went around the table like a shock wave.

"I don't get it," Dr. Maggio said, frowning. "Who's doing this? And why?"

"It's pretty obviously the world government," Richardson said.

"But why?"

"Because they're frightened out of their wits over genetic engineering. They're afraid of what might happen when we succeed."

"I don't believe that."

"Oh no? Well, take a look around you."

Greg Belsen said, "The real question is, what are we going to do about it?"

"What can we do?"

Looking down at the polished tabletop, Dr. Kurtz mumbled in his beard, "Try to get out. Escape."

"How?" Sutherland asked. "Where to?"

Lou said, "They chased me all across the country and back. It may be the world government that's doing this, but they had plenty of Federal marshals helping them."

Dr. Kaufman folded his hands over his midsection. "We're several thousand miles from home, on an island where we'd be very quickly spotted as strangers. Even if we escaped from this villa we wouldn't get very far."

Lou had a sudden thought. "Maybe we don't have to get far. Just to some newsmen. Whoever's behind this, they're trying to keep it quiet. They didn't even notify the local police when they were chasing me. And I didn't hear a word about the Institute's closing on any newscasts."

With a sarcastic grin, Sutherland answered, "So you volunteer to go over the wall and find us a newsman. And he'll tell the world we've been kidnapped or something."

"Something like that," Lou snapped.

"So what?" Sutherland replied. "Suppose the newsman believes you. Suppose, even, he gets to broadcast the story and the world government doesn't stop him. What happens? Some government officials say that he's wrong, he's sensation-mongering. They say that we're a small group of scientists who've been brought here for a special project. End of story. The world doesn't care about twenty-five scientists. We're not news. We're not important people—like Tri-V stars or soccer players."

"Now wait, Charles," Dr. Kaufman said, his eyes brightening. "Christopher may have something. After all, they *have* tried to do this quickly and quietly. Maybe some publicity would break up this whole affair. . . ."

Sutherland made a sour face. "Look at it objectively. We're just a handful of scientists. . . ."

"Oh!" Lou remembered. "They got Dr. Kirby, too."

"Kirby? From Columbia?"

Nodding, Lou answered, "They had him in New York. They were taking him here."

"But he's not here in this villa."

Sutherland waved a finger at them. "You see? There's more to it than just us. I thought so. We're only a part of a bigger picture. And the world government is behind this, whatever it is. Publicity isn't going to hurt them. Either they'll clamp down on any news about this, or they've already figured out what to tell the newsmen."

"Then what can we *do*?" Kaufman demanded.

"Nothing." Sutherland shrugged. "We wait and see what happens. That's all we can do."

Dr. Richardson suddenly asked, "Say, what about Big George? Is he . . ."

"I saw him this morning . . . yesterday, that is," Lou said. "He was scared, but I guess somebody's taking care of him. I hope . . ."

"They can't stick him in a zoo," Greg said. "He'll die of loneliness."

"Or fright."

"Maybe we can ask . . ."

The door from the hall opened and Lou turned to see Mrs. Kaufman standing there, her portly frame tightly wrapped in a nightrobe.

"I finally got the children to sleep," she said to her husband. "Are you coming up soon?"

With a sigh, Dr. Kaufman answered, "In a few minutes, dear."

She nodded and shut the door. Lou stood there by the table, open-mouthed.

Greg said, "Didn't you know? The wives and children were brought here, too. For every married member of the staff. It's a family affair."

Chapter 9

Greg let Lou bunk in with him, in a spacious bedroom on the top floor of the villa. They left the air conditioning off and the balcony doors open. The murmur of the surf quickly lulled them to sleep.

The morning was bright and cloudless. Lou found some clothes in the bedroom closet that fit him: a gaudy disposable shirt and a pair of shorts. It was warm enough to go barefoot.

"There's a Sicilian house staff that will get you more clothes. All you have to do is ask," Greg told him as they went downstairs. "And, man, can they cook! We may not know why we're here, but they're sure treating us right."

The morning was spent exchanging rumors. They were being drafted by the world government for some ultra-secret project. No, there was war brewing between the United States and China and the world government was pulling out the top scientists on both sides to save them from being killed. Nonsense, war is impossible with all nations disarmed; the world government wouldn't allow a war to break out. The *real* story is that there's an epidemic of unknown origin at the Mars base, and we're going to be sent there to find a cure before it wipes out everybody on Mars. Nuts! My brother-in-law's at Mars base and I just got a lasergram from him last week.

The rumors and speculations spiraled hotter and wilder as the sun climbed through the morning sky. But nobody mentioned the simplest explanation: that the government had decided to prevent the work on genetic engineering from being completed. That was too close to home, too plainly possible and painful to be mentioned.

Just before lunchtime, Lou was prowling along the patio that looked out to sea. Several of the older men and their wives were sunning themselves. Lou just couldn't sit still. There had to be something he could do, *something*.

Greg came trotting up the stone stairway that led from the patio to the beach, down below.

"There you are," he said to Lou. "Listen, I've been exploring. Down at the bottom of this picturesque cliff is a picturesque beach. And some of the younger wives and older daughters have found some very picturesque swimsuits and are frolicking on the beach. Beautiful scenery. Including the boss' oldest daughter. How about it?"

The memory of Bonnie stabbed into Lou's mind. "No . . . thanks. I don't feel like it."

Greg shrugged. "Okay, suit yourself. I'll be down there chasing . . . uh, the waves. If anybody's looking for me."

"Sure." Lou turned and started pacing the length of the patio again, trying to think of something useful to do. But he kept seeing Bonnie, crying, scared, and desperate, more afraid of Lou's own anger than anything else, he realized now.

I ought to try to get in touch with her. Tell her it's okay, I'm not sore at her.

He got up and went into the house, looking for one of

the housekeeping staff. Instead he found Kaufman and Sutherland.

"Have you seen Greg Belsen?" Kaufman asked. "They've just told us there's going to be a meeting to explain what this is all about, and we can bring three people. Where is he?"

Lou was about to answer when he remembered that Kaufman's daughter was on the beach. "Greg's . . . uh, he was here a while ago. I don't know where he is now."

Sutherland made a sour face. "The car's right outside, they want us now."

"I'll go," Lou heard himself say.

"You?"

"I'll sit in for Greg."

"But . . ."

"Unless you want to look around for somebody else."

Kaufman glanced unhappily at Sutherland, who was eyeing Lou's vivid shirt and shorts. The two older men were also in sports clothes, but their colors were dark and conservative.

"I could change in two minutes," Lou offered.

"No time to change," Kaufman said. "The car's waiting for us. Come on."

With only a slight grin of satisfaction, Lou went with them to the car. There were two men in the front of the car, both wearing brown uniforms without markings of any kind. They both looked dark, swarthy. And they said nothing.

In the back seat, Sutherland frowned as the car pulled away from the villa. "What do you think this is all about?"

Dr. Kaufman shook his head. "Whatever it is, it will probably be more fantastic than any of the rumors that have been going around."

They drove for nearly an hour down a winding dusty road. Most of the time the road threaded between hills, and there was little to see except the greenery whizzing by. But once in a while they would top a rise and view the sun-dazzled sea stretching off on one side of them, and rich fields of olives and citrus groves on the other side.

Thick clouds began to pile up as they drove on, and by the time they passed the gate of another old villa with its uniformed guards standing at attention, the clouds towered darkly overhead, grumbling and flickering with lightning. It seemed almost as dark as evening, although it was still early afternoon.

There were dozens of cars parked in front of the villa's main entrance. And inside, the old house was filled with men and women, milling around aimlessly, buzzing with conversation.

Lou, Kaufman, and Sutherland stood just inside the front door, gaping at the unexpected crowd.

"That's Margolin, from the Paris Academy," Dr. Kaufman said. "What's he doing here?"

"And Liu from Tokyo," Sutherland added.

"Look . . . Rosenzweig . . . and there's Yossarian!"

"My God, all the top people in the field are here."

Lou recognized some of them, the best-known geneticists and biochemists in the world. He saw no other computer engineers, though.

"Adrian!" called a frail, little man with wispy white hair. "I knew they would bring you here, too."

Kaufman turned and recognized the old man. Both shocked and delighted, he went to him, hands out-stretched. "Max . . . they brought you in on this."

Then Lou realized who he was: Professor DeVreis, the elder statesmen of the world's geneticists, the man who had taught the leaders of the field, like Kaufman, in their university days.

Dr. Sutherland joined them, and soon the three of them formed the nucleus of a growing, grave-faced, head-shaking crowd. Lou stood by the entrance, alone now.

"Do you know any of these people?"

Lou looked up to see a tall, gangly, lantern-jawed fellow his own age standing beside him. He was wearing a baggy suit with full-length trousers and the kind of shoes that you only found in northern hemisphere cities. At second glance, Lou could see that he was trying hard to look calm and unfrightened.

"I don't know many of them personally," Lou answered. Then he pointed out several of the scientists.

His new companion shook his head worriedly. "Geneticists? Biochemists? Why am I here? I'm a nuclear physicist!"

He spoke with a trace of an accent that Lou couldn't pin down.

Now Lou felt equally puzzled. "If it's any consolation, I'm a computer engineer. Um . . . my name's Lou Christopher."

With a toothy grin, he took Lou's offered hand. "I am Anton Kori. I'm from the University of Prague."

"And I'm with the Watson Institute of Genetics . . . or was, that is."

"American?"

Lou nodded. Then he saw that many of the people in the crowd had drinks and sandwiches in their hands. "Looks like lunch is being served someplace around here. Hungry?"

Kori shrugged. "Now that you mention it . . ."

They exchanged stories as they searched through the crowded rooms and finally found the luncheon buffet table.

"Nothing like this has happened in Czechoslovakia in thirty years," Kori said, reaching for a sandwich. "Arrested in the middle of the night and carried off by the police . . . it's like stories my grandfather used to tell us."

Suddenly, his face brightened. "Ah! There are two men I know!"

Lou followed him as he rushed over to a pair of older men standing by the French doors, eating and talking quietly. One of the men was chunky, bald, very fairskinned, dressed in shorts and pullover. The other looked Indian: dark, slim, and intense, slightly Oriental-looking. The plain-gray business suit he wore simply accentuated his exotic looks.

"Clark! Janda!" Kori called out as he rushed up to them.

"Anton," said the chunky man. "What on earth are you doing here? Or for that matter, what are any of us doing here? Do you know?" His accent was unmistakably English.

Kori introduced Lou to Clark Frederick and Ramash Jandawarlu, rocket engineers.

"Rocket engineers?" Lou echoed.

They nodded.

"We were working together—by fax and phone, mostly," said Frederick, "on an improved fusion rocket."

"For interstellar ships," Kori said.

"Interstellar . . . oh, like the probes that were sent out around the turn of the century?" In the back of his mind he was trying to remember whether it was Clark Frederick or Frederick Clark.

"Yes, like the probes, only much better," said Jandawarlu in his reedy voice. "Rocket engines that could propel manned vessels, not merely small instrument probes."

"Manned ships, to the stars?"

"Yes. It would have been something magnificent."

Clark huffed at his co-worker, "You speak as if it's all over for us."

The Indian spread his hands. "We are here. We are not working. I don't think they will allow us to work."

"But who are *they*?" Kori demanded.

Lou said, "The world government. For some reason they've rounded up the world's top geneticists and biochemists . . . and apparently a few rocket people, too."

"But why?"

As if in answer, a voice came from a hidden loud speaker:

"Ladies and gentlemen, if you will kindly assemble in the main salon, we can begin the meeting."

For a second or two the big room was completely silent, everyone stood frozen. There were no sounds from anywhere in the house, no sounds at all except the low grumble of far-off thunder. Then, everybody started talking and moving at once. The hubbub was terrific as more than a hundred men and women poured back into the hall and headed for the villa's largest room.

It wasn't difficult to find the main salon. It was at the end of the front hall, a huge room hung with blue and gold draperies. There were three ornate chandeliers and a half-dozen floor-to-ceiling mirrors set into the walls. The floor was polished wood, for dancing. But there were rows of folding chairs arranged across it now. The far end of the room was bare except for a blank viewscreen on the wall, big enough for a public theater.

Once everyone was inside the room, the doors swung shut and clicked softly. *Nobody in sight, but they're watching us just the same,* Lou thought. And a shiver went through him.

Lou sat with Kori, Frederick, and Janda in one of the rear rows of folding chairs. He saw Kaufman and Sutherland up in the front row, next to Professor DeVreis.

The big viewscreen began to brighten and glow softly. A voice said:

"Gentlemen, you will be addressed by the Honorable Vassily Kobryn, Minister of Security."

The image of Kobryn's heavy, serious face took shape on the screen.

"Russian," muttered Kori.

"Gentlemen," Kobryn said slowly, "it is my unhappy duty to explain to you why you have been taken from your work and your homes to this place. Believe me, the Council of Ministers has thought long and hard before going ahead with this drastic action."

It's going to be bad, Lou realized. *He's preparing us for something even worse than what's happened so far.*

"As you know," Kobryn continued, his face utterly grave, "the government has worked for more than thirty years to make this planet a peaceful, habitable environment. Our efforts have been made extremely difficult by two factors: nationalism and population growth. We believe that we have been successful on both fronts. There are no more national armies and no possibility of a major war between nations. And world population growth has leveled off in the past ten years. Admittedly, twenty-some billions is a much higher figure than anyone would call optimum, but we are managing to provide a livable environment for this population."

"What about the cities?" someone called out.

"Quiet!"

"Let him get to the point."

Kobryn seemed almost glad of the interruption. He answered, "Yes, the cities. I admit that most of the larger cities of the world are completely savage . . . unlivable, by civilized standards. In plain terms, we lost the fight in the giant cities; actually, we started too late. But we have not given up. A considerable portion of our work is being devoted to long-range programs to gradually win the cities back to civilization."

"Why are we here?" a strong voice demanded.

Nodding, Kobryn said, "I am coming to that. You see, we live in a world that is dangerously crowded. There are many who feel that we have passed the point of no return, that our population is too large. They feel that the barbarians of the cities will engulf us all, sooner or later. Even the optimists among us agree that our present population is too large, and we are constantly on the verge of a disaster. If the crops fail anywhere in the world, if a major earthquake or storm escapes our control . . . the repercussions could be tragic for the whole world.

"We have eliminated wars and prevented large-scale starvation. But just barely. We can handle twenty billions of population—*but only if we keep the worldwide society absolutely stable.*"

Kobryn's voice took on a ring of steel at those words. "We must have stability. At any price. All our computer predictions and all our best social planners come to the same conclusion: unless we have stability, this crowded world of ours will crumble into chaos—starvation, disease, war, barbarism. Without stability, we will destroy ourselves and poison this planet completely."

There was a long, silent moment while Kobryn stared at them from the viewscreen, letting his words sink in. No one in the audience spoke. The quiet was broken only by somebody's cough and the nervous shuffling of feet.

"The price we must pay for stability is progress. You and your work are part of that price."

Now everyone stirred. A sort of collective sigh went through the big room, almost a gasp but not strong enough. More worried and afraid than shocked or angry.

Kobryn went on, "Most of you are geneticists and

biochemists. You have proven in recent experiments that you can alter the genetic material in a fertilized ovum, so that you can control the physical and mental characteristics of the baby that is ultimately born. Professor DeVreis, you yourself told me that within a few years, you could produce a superman. . . ."

"Yes," DeVreis agreed in his rickety, aged voice. "A superman . . . or a zombie, a slave with bulging muscles and just enough intelligence to follow orders."

"Just so," Kobryn said, his face expressionless. "In either case, the result would be a complete shattering of society's stability. We cannot allow this to happen."

"Can't allow . . ."

"What does he mean?"

"You can't stop science!"

"Gentlemen, please!" Kobryn raised his voice. "Think a moment! No matter how attractive the picture you have of raising a race of supermen, you must realize that it will never come to pass. Who will be the first superman? How will you select? Don't you understand that twenty billions of people will bury you in their stampede to have their children made into godlings? Or worse still, they might slaughter the first few supermen you produce in an insane fit of fear and jealousy."

"No, it wouldn't happen that way. . . ."

"We wouldn't let . . ."

"No matter how you look at it, any large-scale tampering with mankind's genetic heritage will destroy society as we know it. Believe me! We have spent a year and more examining this question. The best computers and social engineers in the world have labored on the problem. Our world needs stability. Genetic engineering is a de-stabilizing element, a wild card that will destroy society. The government cannot permit this."

"But it will create a better society! A world of supermen!"

Kobryn shook his head. "No! It will create chaos. Look at what happened in the last century, when vast groups of peoples suddenly became aware that they could be free of the social systems that had enslaved them. When the last vestiges of the European empires were removed from Asia and Africa, when the American Negro and the world's youth realized that they had political power, what happened? Was there a peaceful march toward a happy society? No, nothing of the sort. There were wars and revolutions, riots and assassinations—it took nearly the entire twentieth century before an equilibrium was reached. And for most of that time the world population was below five billions!

"Now we have in our grasp this possibility of genetic engineering, the possibility of making our children into godlings—or slaves. Do you think the people of the world will stand patiently in line, waiting for you to work your miracle for them? Don't you understand that many would-be tyrants would use your knowledge to produce the zombies Professor DeVreis spoke of? In a world of twenty billions, we would never recover from such a violent upset to the social order. There would be no new equilibrium, only chaos. Our world would come crashing down in anarchy and rioting. Your laboratories would be destroyed, and you yourselves would be torn to pieces by the mobs."

There were a few halfhearted protests from the audience.

Finally Kobryn said grimly, "The government has decided that all research in genetic engineering must be stopped. Therefore, we have brought the leaders in this work to this meeting. You and your colleagues—some two thousand scientists, in all—are to be exiled. . . ."

"Exiled!"

"What?"

"But you can't . . ."

"Permanently exiled, together with your immediate families, aboard an orbital satellite that has been set aside especially for you."

Kaufman was on his feet. "You can't do that! We're citizens and we have constitutional rights!"

"The world constitution specifically gives the Legislative Assembly the power to suspend constitutional guarantees in cases of extreme emergency," Kobryn replied. "Last week, the Assembly voted and approved your exile. The World Court has reviewed the situation and found that we are acting in a perfectly legal manner."

Kaufman stood there for a moment, hand up as if there was another point he wanted to make. Then slowly, like an inflated doll collapsing from a leak, he crumpled back onto his chair.

"No one regrets this drastic action more than the Council of Ministers," Kobryn said to the silent audience. "You men and women represent the world's best scientists. But for the safety and stability of the world's billions, a few thousand must be sacrificed. Your living conditions aboard the satellite, though rather crowded, will be as pleasant and even luxurious as they can be made to be. We do not wish to harm you. We have tried to find an alternate solution to the problem. There is none. And it is absolutely imperative that your work in genetic engineering is not allowed to affect mankind. We are trying to avert disaster. I hope you understand."

"Filthy liar," Kori muttered.

Frederick stood up and called out, "My name is Clark Frederick. I'm neither a geneticist nor a biochemist, but a rocket engineer. A few of my colleagues are here too. Are we included in this exile? And if so, why?"

Kobryn glanced away, at something or somebody out of camera range. Then he looked down, as if quickly reading something.

"Ah. Dr. Frederick, yes. You and several other scientists and engineers who have been working on interstellar rockets are also included—I regret to say. It was decided that your work could also upset the stability of society, and . . ." Kobryn shrugged, as if to say, *You know the rest.*

Frederick's face turned red with anger. "How in blazes can rockets to Alpha Centauri or Barnard's Star upset the social equilibrium on Earth?"

"Let me explain," said Kobryn. "If the masses of people on Earth believed that starships could transport them to new worlds, new planets of other stars, there might be millions who would seek out this new frontier. As you know full well, only a pitiful handful could ever hope to travel in a starship. It's much too expensive for true colonization."

"Of course. Everyone knows that," Frederick replied.

"No, not everyone. The great masses of people would expect your starships to transport them to new worlds, where they could begin new lives, free of Earth. And when we would tell them that this is impossible, they would not believe us. The result would be protests, riots, uprisings." Kobryn shook his head. "We cannot permit it. I am truly sorry."

Frederick sat down.

"Besides," Kori said to him, "they get to spend the money we were using on themselves."

Professor DeVreis was up again. "Minister Kobryn, you have sentenced several thousand men, women, and children to permanent exile. We naturally reject this decision in its entirety. It is completely antithetical to the spirit of the world government and the liberty of mankind. We demand a fair and open hearing before the Council of Ministers, the Assembly, and the World Court."

Kobryn's face hardened. His giant image loomed over the frail old man. "You do not understand. The decision has been made. It is final. There is no appeal. We will begin transporting you to the orbital station tomorrow."

The viewscreen went blank, leaving them all sitting there stunned into silence.

Chapter 10

By mid-afternoon the next day, a dozen men and their families had been taken from the villa by silent men in unmarked uniforms. The Kaufmans and the Sutherlands were the first to go.

Take the leaders first and the rest are easy to handle, Lou said to himself.

He wandered through the villa aimlessly. Everybody seemed to be in shock. People huddled in small groups, family groups mostly, talking in low and frightened tones. Lou was alone, a complete outsider. No family, not even his girl.

Again and again a shining black minibus would pull up the driveway and two men would get out. Unsmilingly, they would go through the rambling old house until they found the person they were looking for. A few moments of conversation, and then a family would follow the men out to the driveway, wide-eyed and shaken, to be bundled into the minibus and whisked away.

Lou stood on the balcony above the main entrance and watched one of the buses grind up the driveway, swaying top-heavily, and then swing out onto the road kicking up a plume of dust. It had showered the evening before, but the land was bone dry again this afternoon. Lou looked up. The sky was bright, but off on the sea horizon there were black clouds building up again.

A sleek little turbocar was coming down the road toward the villa, top down, two men in the front seat. It swung into the driveway in a flurry of dust and skid-screeching wheels, and pulled up to the entrance. Sitting next to the driver was the Norseman. He glanced up at the balcony and grinned.

"Very cooperative of you to be waiting for us," he called to Lou. "Will you join us, please?"

Despite himself, Lou felt startled. *It's my turn already.*

"Mr. Christopher," the Norseman said, "you won't try anything foolish, I hope."

Lou glared at him. Without a word of answer he turned and went inside to find the stairs that led down to the front hall.

The sky was filling up with thunderheads and the late afternoon sunlight had that threatening, electrical yellow cast, with the damp sweet smell of an impending storm. It was cool and exhilarating in the back seat of the convertible, the wind clean and strong, tearing at your hair and clothes, making you squint your eyes and press your lips shut as the car roared along. They had come down the dusty coast road and turned onto a broad plastisteel throughway. For many miles the convertible was the only car on the road, but gradually the traffic built up. Now Lou could see the towers of a city off among the distant hills, and big trailer trucks were whizzing along beside them on air-cushion jets, streaking toward that city.

Lou knew better than to ask questions. Conversation from the back seat of the speeding car was next to impossible anyhow, even if they could or would answer. He simply sat there, enjoying the wind and watching the clouds blot out the sunshine and make the countryside look dark and gloomy.

Take a good look, he told himself. *It's probably the last time you'll ever see any of this.*

They barely beat the rain. The convertible, still top down, threaded through a maze of elevated highways at the city's outskirts and then dove into a tunnel as the first big drops splattered on Lou's bare legs. The tunnel must have had acoustic insulation of some sort, because even though the car didn't slow down, the roar of its turbine didn't echo and thunder the way it would have in a normal tunnel. They pulled into an underground garage and stopped in front of an unmarked doorway. The Norseman got out and held the door open for Lou. As soon as they were both out of the car, the driver revved the engine and drove off.

The Norseman led Lou into the building, down a hallway, and to an elevator that was waiting with its door open. He was watching Lou warily, and stayed slightly behind him, out of reach, as Lou stepped into the elevator cab. Then he walked in, flicked a finger at the topmost button on the control panel, and the doors swished shut.

As the elevator slid smoothly upward, the Norseman turned to Lou. "I understand that you people are being moved to a satellite."

"We're being exiled," Lou said, feeling his anger returning.

"Yes, so I heard."

"For life."

The Norseman nodded.

"Whole families. Several thousand people."

"I know . . . I'm sorry."

"Did you know it when you brought me here from the States?"

He shook his head.

"Would it have made any difference to you if you had known what they were going to do with us?"

The Norseman looked at Lou. "I was only doing my job. . . ."

"Would it have made any difference?" Lou insisted.

"Well . . . no, I don't suppose it would have."

"Then don't tell me you're sorry."

"But . . ."

"Stuff it."

The elevator stopped and the doors slid open. Lou had expected to see a hallway, a corridor. But instead he stepped directly into a huge, sumptuously furnished room. Thick red carpeting, a long conference table surrounded by tall comfortable chairs, all in the rich brown of real wood. Two of the walls were a smooth cream color, a third was splashed with an abstract mural. The far end of the room was plastiglass, but all Lou could see through the windows was mist and the streaks of raindrops. There was a massive desk near the windows, its black leather swivel chair unoccupied at the moment. The air felt cool and clean, the room even seemed to smell of authority and power.

"You will wait here," the Norseman said.

Lou turned back and realized that his escort hadn't

gotten out of the elevator. The doors slid shut with a soft sigh.

Completely puzzled, Lou walked across the big room to the windows. His steps made no sound on the luxurious carpet. It was raining so hard now that the city was only a blurred gray outline. Then Lou heard a door open. He turned and saw a smiling middle-aged man enter. He was shorter than Lou, stocky but not yet turning soft. His hair was still thick and dark, although his forehead had started to recede. He wore a light business suit.

"Mr. Christopher, a pleasure to meet you," he said, gesturing toward one of the plush chairs by the desk.

He spoke with a European accent of some sort, Lou couldn't place it. And Lou had the feeling that he had seen this man before, on Tri-V newscasts, perhaps.

"My name is Rolf Bernard," he said, taking the chair behind the desk. "That probably means nothing to you. The Finance Ministry is often behind the news, but seldom in it."

"Of course," Lou said. "The Minister of Finance."

Bernard smiled. "You know my name? I am flattered."

"I . . . uh . . ."

"Yes. You are wondering why you are here. It is very simple. Not everyone in the Council of Ministers is a monster, Mr. Christopher. The decision to exile you and your colleagues was not a unanimous one, I assure you."

Lou felt more puzzled than ever.

"Mr. Christopher, I will come directly to the point. There is nothing I can do to save your friends from exile. Even as Minister of Finance, I am powerless to stop this cruel and degrading action." He hesitated a moment, then added, "At this time."

Lou felt his innards tighten. "What do you mean?"

"I am totally against this decision to exile the geneticists," Bernard said, his voice firm. "There are a few others on the Council of Ministers who agree with me. We do not have sufficient power to reverse the decision of the Council, but we will not sit by idly and watch this happen without taking steps to correct the situation."

"But, I don't see . . ."

"How can you see? No one is certain of anything at this point in time. Except for this: I am certain that a few of my fellow Ministers will work together to free your comrades and bring justice out of this exilement."

Lou nodded.

"Now then, as a more concrete action, I am prepared to offer you an escape from exile."

"Escape?"

"Reprieve, parole, whatever word you wish to use."

"What do you mean?"

Smiling broadly now, Bernard said, "There is no way for me to save any of the geneticists or biochemists. Not now, at any rate. But you are not a geneticist nor a biochemist. I can take . . . eh, certain action, that will remove your name from the list of those who are to be exiled."

"What? How . . ."

Bernard stopped him with an upthrust hand. "Never mind how. Believe me when I say that it can be done. You need not be exiled to the satellite station. There are a few others, also, whom I can slip out of the lists and save."

"But the geneticists?"

Shaking his head sadly, "Nothing can be done to save them, at present. Rest assured, they will be comfortable enough in the satellite. Physically, at least. And also be assured that powerful men, myself included, will be working night and day to rescue them and return them to their rightful places here on Earth."

Lou sank back in his chair. His head was starting to spin. Everything was happening so fast.

"Now then," Bernard went on, "you realize of course that your Institute has been permanently closed, as have all the leading genetics laboratories around the world. There are still plenty of geneticists and biochemists, plenty of working laboratories, left on our planet. But the best people, the leaders, the *elite*—they have been exiled. In this manner, the government hopes to stifle the progress of your science."

"In the name of stability," Lou muttered.

"Yes. You understand, I trust, that the government will not allow you to begin work at any of the genetics laboratories that have been left open. If they learn that you are working in this field, they will take you again and exile you. Or perhaps kill you."

"But . . ."

The big smile returned, and somehow it began to look slightly wolfish to Lou. "Hear me out. I have taken the liberty of starting a small genetics laboratory of my own —safely tucked away from prying eyes. You and several others whom I am able to save from exile can work there.

I will try to bring some of the best geneticists and biochemists available to work with you. They will not be the leaders of their fields, of course, but they will be the best of those who have escaped exilement. Your work can go on while we try to end the exile of your friends."

Lou could hardly believe what he was hearing. "After all that's happened over the past few days . . . it's . . . well, meeting a sane man in the government is a jolt."

Bernard laughed. "It is not so much that I am sane; I am unafraid. The others on the Council fear your science. They seek safety in stability and order. I welcome change. I welcome your science. Without progress, the world will sink into barbarism."

For the first time since the marshal had arrested him, Lou felt himself really relaxing. He grinned at the Minister of Finance. "You don't know how important those words are."

Nodding, Bernard added, "I have also taken the liberty of bringing some of the equipment and animal stock from various laboratories to my new location. I understand one of your animals is a gorilla that can talk! Absolutely marvelous!"

"Big George," Lou murmured. "He's okay."

"Yes, the gorilla is healthy." Bernard seemed amused, "Apparently he was asking for you."

Lou nodded.

"Now you must realize," Bernard went on, hunching forward at the desk, his face grown serious, "that my laboratory is a private, even a secret affair. None of the other Ministers knows about this. It is located on an island, and once you are safely there, you will not be allowed to leave. Until, that is, the entire business of the exile is settled."

"But why secret?" Lou asked. "Why don't you tell the world about the exile? Why keep everything hushed up? That's just what the government wants."

"My dear young friend, this is a very complicated business, and the stakes we are playing for are extremely high. If we make the smallest mistake, we will lose everything. You must trust me to do what is best. At the proper time, the world will learn what has happened, I assure you."

"Well," Lou said. "Okay, I guess you know more about this than I do."

"Fine!" Bernard started beaming again. "Now, is there anything else you will need to continue your work? We have already dismantled your computer and are bringing it to the new laboratory."

Before he realized what he was saying, Lou blurted, "There's a computer programmer—her name's Bonnie Sterne. She . . ."

"You want her at the new laboratory?"

"Yes, but she's not one of the exiles. She's in Albuquerque. And she might not want to come. . . ."

Bernard waved his objections away. "She will come. I know women a little better than you do. If we tell her that you are safe and want her to be with you, she will come."

Lou felt almost numb as he left Bernard's office. The Norseman met him at the elevator again and guided him back to the waiting car. Lou felt as if his mind was somehow stuck in neutral gear. So much had happened. So much to absorb.

As he sat in the back seat of the car, driving through the chilling late afternoon rain, he tried to tell himself that he should feel happy. At least Bernard was on his side, on the side of justice and reason. *Okay, so living on this island will be an exile of sorts, too. But at least you'll be working, and Bonnie'll be there. What more do you want?*

But somehow it didn't work. Lou didn't feel happy at all, just vaguely uneasy, wary. And then he realized that he didn't have the faintest idea of where they were driving him.

Chapter 11

The new laboratory was on an island, all right. A Pacific island, Lou guessed, from the number of Orientals around the place. Most of the office people were Chinese or Malay. Half the computer programmers were Japanese.

Lou had been flown in the same day he had talked to Minister Bernard. They wasted no time. Anton Kori was on the plane with him, the only other passenger. Most of the trip was made at night, so neither Kori nor Lou could tell where they were going, except that they had been heading roughly southeastward when the sun set. The crew—two Arabic-looking pilots and a black engineer—said nothing to them.

Lou and Kori were separated at landing. A Chinese, about Lou's own age, drove him in an open-topped turbowagon from the jet landing pad through a narrow dark road that seemed to be cut into a jungle. He pulled up at a plastic prefab dormitory building and showed Lou to a room on the ground floor. Not much furniture, but the bed was comfortable and Lou was asleep before he had even taken off his shoes.

The next morning, breakfast was brought to him by the same Chinese.

"The director of the laboratory asked me to convey his greetings to you," he said. "He requests that you enjoy yourself this morning in any way you desire. He will meet you here for lunch. At noon precisely."

Lou glanced at his wristwatch.

"I took the liberty of setting it correctly for you."

Looking up sharply at him, Lou asked, "While I was asleep?"

The Chinese nodded, with the faintest trace of a smile on his otherwise impassive face.

So Lou spent the morning walking around the island. It was small, no more than a half-dozen kilometers long, and half that wide. It was really nothing more than a pair of heavily-wooded hills poking out of the water. The trees were palms and other tropical species that Lou couldn't identify.

The sun was hot, but the ocean breeze was beautiful. The place really was a tropical island paradise.

There were lovely white sand beaches all the way around the island, and a coral reef further out where the surf broke, except for a small inlet at one end. Lou saw a fair-sized, air-cushion ship resting in the gentle swells of the inlet. There was a dock there and a few plain white buildings. Slightly away from the buildings was the jet landing pad, a square of well-kept grass. The plane was gone now. There was no runway for bigger jets anywhere on the island; the vertical landing type were the only planes that could come down.

The dormitory building was at the opposite end of the island, connected to the inlet by the single road out through the trees. In the middle of the island, set into the fairly flat area between the two hills, were the laboratory buildings.

The labs were tucked away in the shade of tall trees. There were six buildings in all, filled with the bustling, nearly frantic action of men unpacking huge crates of equipment and working hard to set them up as quickly as possible. Their shouting and hammering drove Lou away very quickly. He only stayed long enough to make certain that they weren't damaging the equipment that they were handling. They weren't. They knew what they were doing.

And then, as he passed between two of the labs, Lou heard a scratchy hoarse voice calling:

"Uncle Lou!"

He looked up and saw Big George standing erect, his huge arms upraised so that his hands rested on the top of the nine-foot wire screen fence that stood between them. The fence bulged dangerously under his weight.

"Hey, Georgy!" Lou felt his face stretch into its biggest smile in days as he ran toward the fence.

The gorilla jumped up and down and slapped his sides with excitement. "Uncle Lou! Uncle Lou!"

"Georgy, you okay?" Lou asked as he reached the fence.

"Yes, yes. Strangers scared me at first, but they are very nice to me. It was lonesome, though, without you or any of my other friends."

"Well, I'm here now. Everything's going to be okay, Georgy. Come on down to that gate over there and I'll get you out of this compound."

Big George lumbered along the fence, knuckles on the ground. Lou saw that the gate had no lock on it, just a simple latch. With a shrug, he opened it.

George lurched out and grabbed Lou in his immense arms.

"Hey! Careful!" Lou laughed as George lifted him off his feet, strong enough to crush him, gentle enough to handle an equal amount of nitroglycerin without danger.

Lou pounded the gorilla's massive hairy shoulders happily. The warmth of his body, even his scent, carried the impression of huge jungle strength. And if the gorilla could have laughed or even smiled, he would have right then.

A pistol shot cracked nearby. Startled, George jerked and nearly let Lou fall. Lou saw sudden fear in the gorilla's eyes, then turned to see some sort of uniformed guard pointing a pistol at them.

"Stop! Put that man down!" the guard yelled—from a safe distance away. He was wearing a khaki-colored shirt and shorts, with a little cap on his head and that big gun in his wavering hand.

"Shut up," Lou snapped. "And put that stupid gun away. We're old friends. He's not hurting me."

The guard's mouth dropped open.

"Let me down," Lou said softly to George. The gorilla stood him carefully on his feet.

Walking to the wide-eyed guard, Lou said, "Put that gun away and don't let me catch you doing anything that hurts that gorilla or frightens him in any way. Do you understand?"

"I . . . I thought . . ."

"You thought wrong. Big George wouldn't hurt anybody—unless they scared him so badly that he lashed out in fright."

"I was only . . ."

"You were wrong. Now get out of here."

"Yessir." The guard turned and walked away, fumbling the gun back into the holster strapped to his hip.

Lou stayed with Big George until lunchtime—but inside the relative safety of the wire screen that marked off the gorilla's compound. *Too many people out there who've been frightened by bad movies. And too many guns.* The compound was wide and wild, Lou saw. George had plenty of room, big trees, a stream, even the slope of one of the hills to climb.

"You'd better stay inside," Lou said as he left the gorilla at the gate, "until the people around here get to know you better. I wouldn't want you to get into trouble."

"I know," George whispered. "I'll be good."

Lou smiled at him. "Sure you will. I'll see you soon."

Lou walked briskly back toward his quarters, knowing that George would spend the better part of the afternoon feeding himself. It took a huge supply of fruits and vegetables to keep a gorilla satisfied. By the time Lou approached the white prefab building, he felt sweaty and uncomfortable. It was beginning to get really hot, and the breeze had slackened.

The turbowagon was sitting in front of the dorm, with a driver wearing the same sort of khaki uniform that the gun-waving guard had worn. The driver also had a holster strapped on.

In the back seat an older man was reading some papers. His face was mild and milky white, with a high balding forehead and thin sandy hair that had started to turn gray. He looked slim to Lou, and was probably getting near-sighted, judging from the way he held the papers close to his nose. He wore a starched white shirt, short-sleeved, and full-length trousers.

He looked up as Lou's sandals crunched on the gravel of the driveway.

"Ah . . . Mr. Christopher."

Lou nodded and put on a smile as he walked up to the wagon.

"I'm Donald Marcus, the head of the laboratory." Marcus put his hand out and Lou shook it. The grip was limp, almost slippery.

"Get in and we'll go down to the lab area. I want you to see the computer set-up before we have lunch."

Lou climbed up into the wagon and sat beside his new boss.

"By the way," Marcus said as they drove off, "did you know that you're three minutes late?"

Without even blinking, Lou snapped back, "My guard must've set my watch wrong."

Marcus looked a little startled, but said nothing.

The computer was housed in a building of its own, off to one side of the lab complex and not far from Big George's compound.

Inside the one-story building was chaos. Workmen were uncrating bulky consoles, ripping off the protective plastic coverings, leaving huge gobs of the spongy foam heaped all over the floor. Carpenters were putting up partitions with whirring drills and power saws. Someone was pounding on a wall someplace. Everyone was talking, calling back and forth, shouting orders or responses, mostly in sing-song Chinese. Lou was nearly run down by four men who, with backs bent and heads down, were wheeling in the massive main control desk at breakneck speed from the open double doors at one end of the building.

It was hot and sticky, and the room smelled of new plastic and machine oil. Lou felt perspiration trickling down his body.

"Most of these components," Marcus yelled over the din, "come from your computer system at the Genetics Institute."

Lou nodded but kept his eyes on the nearest workmen, who were busily laying a heavy cable across the floor.

"We brought the logic circuits and the whole memory bank."

"What about the voice circuits and input software?" Lou shouted.

Marcus lowered his voice a notch. "Um, we didn't bring the voice circuits or the vocal input units. You'll have to type your inputs to the computer and get the replies on the viewscreen or printer, just like any ordinary machine."

"What? How come?"

Marcus avoided Lou's eyes. "Well, we didn't have the time or the transportation capacity to take everything. Besides . . ." his voice lower, so that Lou had to bend down a bit to hear him, "with all these Chinks around as workmen and technicians, if they heard a computer talk they'd probably get scared out of their skulls. They'd think it was devils or something supernatural."

Lou stared at him. "You're kidding. Nobody's . . ."

Marcus stopped him with an upraised hand. "No, I'm serious. Sure, we've got some good people on the technical staff, but the hired hands are straight from the hill country, believe me. My own driver—he's a great mechanic, don't get me wrong. But he keeps some powdered bones in a bag around his neck. Claims they keep evil spirits away."

When they went outside and climbed back into the car, Lou took a careful look. Sure enough, the driver had a thin leather thong tied around the brown skin of his neck, with a tiny bag at the end of it.

They had lunch on the veranda of Marcus' quarters, a house made of real stone and wood, with a red tile roof that overhung the walls by several feet and made welcome shade against the heat of the sun. The house was atop the hill that overlooked the little blue-water inlet, and the breeze from the ocean made it very pleasant on the veranda. Lou leaned back in a wicker chair, watching the moisture beading on the outside of his iced drink, listening to the songbirds in the flowering bushes that surrounded the house.

"A month ago," Marcus was saying, "this was the only house on the island. By the end of this week, we'll have more than a hundred people here—twenty of them scientists, like yourself."

"I'm not a scientist," Lou said automatically. "I'm a computer engineer."

Marcus smiled wanly. "Yes, I know. But anybody who

understands this genetics business looks like a scientist to me. I'm a civil engineer, by training. Right now, I guess I'm just a straw boss."

The young Malay driver served them lunch on a round bamboo table, his little bag of magic dangling between Lou and Marcus whenever he bent over to put something on the table.

"Minister Bernard's plan," Marcus said as they ate, "is to carry on the work that was going on at the top genetics labs."

Lou shook his head. "Twenty men can't do the work of two thousand. Especially when those two thousand were the best men in their fields."

Marcus chewed thoughtfully on a mouthful of food. He swallowed and then said, "I know it won't be easy. We've brought some good people here, but you're perfectly right, they're not the best. And we couldn't bring too many of them either, without the government catching on to what we're trying to do."

"Just what is it that you *are* trying to do?"

"Exactly what I told you," Marcus said, concentrating his gaze on a leaf of salad that was eluding his fork. "We're going to continue the work you were doing at the Institute. We're going to complete it, and show the world that we can alter a human embryo deliberately, and safely. Once we've announced that news, and told the people that the government tried to prevent this work from being completed, the government will have to relent and allow your friends to return to their homes and their work."

Lou felt an old excitement tingling through his body.

"The next step in evolution," he said so softly that it was almost a reverent whisper. "Man's conscious improvement of his own mind and body."

Marcus leaned back in his chair.

"It's criminal," Lou flared, "for the government to stop this work! In a generation or two we could be turning out people who are physically and mentally perfect!"

Smiling, Marcus said, "Yes, we can. And we will, if you can do your part in this job. You realize, don't you, that you're the most important human being on Earth?"

Chapter 12

Lou felt physically staggered. He stared at Marcus, who was smiling easily at him.

"Me? What are you talking about?"

"It's very simple," Marcus explained. "All of the world's top geneticists and biochemists have been put into exile. They're being shipped up to their satellite prison right now. Of all the top men working on genetic engineering, you're the only one we've been able to save."

"But . . ."

"Oh, sure, we've rounded up a few of the second-string people, and we've brought in a couple of young pups, bright boys, but the ink is still wet on their diplomas. You're the only experienced top-flight man we have."

"But I'm only a computer engineer."

Nodding, "Maybe, but your work is the key to the whole project. You've got the computer coding system in your hands. Unless we can get the computer to handle all of the thousands of variables that are involved in any tinkering with the genes, we don't dare try to do anything. It would be too dangerous."

Lou agreed, "Yeah . . . you've got to have the computer plot out all the possible side effects of any change you make. Otherwise you'd never know if you were making the zygote better or worse."

"Right," Marcus said. "And you're the only man who was close enough to the geneticists to really understand what the computer coding system must be. We've checked all across the world, believe me. None of the other labs were as close to success as your Institute. And none of them had a computer system as sophisticated as yours. So that makes you the key man. The fate of your friends—the fate of the whole world—is in your hands."

Grinning foolishly, Lou said, "Well . . . it's really in Ramo's hands. Ramo's got the whole thing wrapped up in his memory banks."

Marcus tensed in his chair. "The whole thing?"

Lou nodded. "All I've got to do is run through the programs and de-bug them. Then we'll be ready for the first experiments. Take me a few weeks, at most."

"This is critically important to us," Marcus said. "I don't want you to rush it. I want it done right."

Feeling a little irritated, Lou said, "It's almost finished. In a few weeks, we'll be ready."

"You'll be able to scan the zygote's genetic structure, spot any defects, plot out the proper corrective steps, and predict the results?"

"To twenty decimal places," Lou insisted. "And it'll all be done in less than a minute of computer time."

"If you can do that . . ."

"*When* we can do that," Lou corrected, "we'll be able to mend any genetic defects in the zygote and make each embryo genetically perfect. Ultimately, we'll be able to produce a race of people with no physical defects and an intelligence level way beyond the genius class."

"Yes," Marcus said. "Ultimately."

Lou sat back, Marcus smiled pleasantly and sipped his drink. Then Lou noticed, through the chirping of the songbirds, the drone of a jet high overhead. Marcus heard it too. He looked up at the silvery speck with its pencil-thin line of white contrail speeding along behind it.

Glancing down at his wristwatch, Marcus said, "That's our next supply shipment. Your programmer friend should be on that plane."

"Bonnie?"

Marcus nodded. "I understand she's quite a lovely girl." He grinned at Lou.

Pushing his chair from the table, Lou got up. "I'll go down to meet her at the landing pad."

"Sure, go right ahead. Her quarters are in the same building as yours. She's on the second floor."

"Okay. Fine." Lou started toward the front of the house. Suddenly, he didn't want to be bothered by Marcus or anyone else. He just wanted to see Bonnie.

"I'm afraid the car's already down there," Marcus said, trailing along behind Lou. "You'll have to walk it."

"That's okay. See you later."

He left Marcus standing in front of the house and started down the dirt road toward the harbor area. The jet sounded closer now, and Lou could see it circling, still pretty high out over the sea.

From behind him he heard the whine of another turbowagon. Turning, he saw Kori jouncing in the back seat as the wagon worked slowly down the rutted road toward the harbor. Lou waved and Kori yelled for the driver to stop. They lurched off together toward the landing pad.

"Going to meet the plane?" Lou asked.

"Yes. They're bringing some equipment in for me. And some data tapes from *Starfarer* that came in just before I was arrested."

"The interstellar probe?"

The road leveled out and they picked up speed. Light and shadows flickered across Kori's face as they drove past a stand of tall palms.

"Yes. If everything was working right, these tapes might have close-up pictures of Alpha Centauri on them."

"Really? But I didn't see anything in the newscasts about it. . . ."

The road wound along the edge of the harbor now, and the driver pushed the turbine to top speed. There was no other traffic. The wind tore at Kori and Lou in the back seat.

"The government kept it quiet," Kori hollered back. "Remember what Kobryn said, back in Sicily? Alpha Centauri is a threat to the stability of the world," Kori laughed bitterly.

The car screeched to a halt alongside the landing pad. Billowing dust enveloped them for a moment. Blinking and coughing, Lou jumped out of the car and walked clear of the slowly-settling dust cloud. Kori came up beside him, walking in a slow gangling gait.

"Are you going to be working on the probe data? Is that what Marcus wants you to do?"

Kori made a little shrug. "He said I can work on analyzing the data. But what he really wants me to do is to make some nuclear explosives for him."

"Explosives? You mean bombs?"

"No, no, nothing so big," Kori answered, grinning. "Just little things, toys, really. The kind that engineers use on construction jobs. Why, if you exploded one of them in a city, it would hardly take out a building."

The plane was circling low now, its jets roaring in their ears. Lou watched as its wings spread straight out for landing and the jet pods swiveled to the vertical position. Slowly the plane settled on its screaming exhaust of hot gases, flattening the grass beneath it. Through shimmering heat waves Lou saw the plane's wheels touch the ground and the weight of the jet settle on them. Then the turbine's bellowing whine died off, like some supernatural demon melting away.

Lou took his hands down from his ears; they were ringing slightly.

The hatch of the jet popped open, and a three-step metal ladder slid to the ground. A broad-shouldered young man stepped out first, then turned around and reached up to help the next passenger. It was Bonnie.

She was wearing shorts and a sleeveless blouse. Her hair was pinned up the way she usually wore it at work. Her face looked grave, utterly serious, perhaps a little scared.

Lou felt something jump inside of him, and then he was running toward her, calling to her.

"Bonnie! Bonnie!"

She looked up, saw him, and smiled. Lou ran up to her, past the guy who had helped her down the steps. He wrapped her in his arms and swung her around off her feet.

"Am I glad to see you! You came! You did come."

She looked surprised and happy and worried, all at the same time. "Lou . . . you're all right. They didn't hurt you or anything. . . ."

"I'm fine, now that you're here."

Without ever letting go of her arm, Lou took Bonnie's one travel bag from the Chinese guard who was unloading the baggage and started walking her back toward the car. Kori was still standing beside the wagon, so Lou introduced them.

Kori said, "Why don't you two drive back to the dormitory? I'm sure you'll want to get unpacked and settled in your room, Miss Sterne. It'll be some time before all my junk is unloaded from the plane. Lou, if you'll just send the car back here. . . ."

"Fine, fine, I'll do that." Lou was grinning broadly as he helped Bonnie into the back seat of the car and got in beside her.

She was very quiet as they drove away from the pad and the harbor. Lou chattered about what a beautiful island it was, and how good it was to see her again. All Bonnie did was to nod once in a while. By the time Lou had carried her travel bag up to the door of her room, his own joy at being with her had simmered down to the point where he could see that something was wrong.

There were no locks on the dormitory doors, only latches that could be pushed home from the inside. So Lou opened her door and gestured her into the room.

Bonnie walked in and looked around.

"This will be my room?"

"Right. It's not much, I know, but . . ."

She went to the window and looked out. Turning back to him, she asked, "And your room is in the same building?"

"Downstairs."

"How many other women are in this building?"

Lou shrugged. "This whole second floor is for women, I think. And there are a few married couples living on the island. They've got their own houses, though."

"I see."

"Look, Bonnie, you're not sore about what I said when those Federal marshals arrested me, are you? I was scared, and surprised. . . ."

Her face softened a little. "No, it's not that, Lou."

He walked over to her. "Then what's wrong? Why'd you come if you didn't . . ."

"Why'd I come?" She almost laughed at him. "I didn't get much choice. Two men picked me up at the office where I had just started working and packed me off. That was it. No questions, no explanations. Just enough time to pack one bag. That's all."

"They didn't tell you . . ."

"Nothing. In fact, I'm still not sure of what's going on."

Lou sank down into the nearest chair. "But Bernard must have . . ."

Bonnie knelt down beside him and put her hands in his. "Lou, I'm sorry. When I saw you there by the plane, all of a sudden I thought it was *you* that had me kidnapped."

"You haven't been kidnapped!"

"I haven't been invited to the prince's ball."

He laughed with her.

"Lou, what's going on? Is everything going crazy?"

Shaking his head, he tried to explain it as carefully as he could. The exile. Minister Bernard's offer to help. The work that was going to be done on this island.

Finally, she understood. "You mean we're going to stay here . . . indefinitely? As long as they want us to? We can't get off?"

He looked into her pearl gray eyes and really didn't care about politics or exilements or science or anything else. But he forced himself to answer, "We stay until we've finished the work that was going on at the Institute. When we show the world that genetic engineering can be done, then there's no more point in keeping Kaufman and the others in exile."

"But that could take years," Bonnie said.

"It won't be that long."

She looked away from him, off toward the window, like a prisoner who's suddenly realized that the outside world is forever barred away.

"I shouldn't have asked them to bring you here," Lou said.

She didn't answer.

"Bonnie . . . if you had known . . . if they told you that you'd have to live on this island until the project is finished . . . with me . . . would you have come?"

She turned back to look at him, and there were tears in her eyes. "I don't know, Lou. I just don't know."

Chapter 13

There are more than three hundred trillion cells in the human body. Counting ten cells per second, it would take more than a million years to count them all. In each cell there are forty-six chromosomes; under the microscope they look long and threadlike, and they've often been described as "strings of beads." Each "bead" is an individual gene, and altogether there are some forty thousand genes in any human cell.

The zygote—the fertilized egg cell that develops into an embryo and within nine months into a baby—contains about forty thousand genes, just like any human cell. Half this number come from each parent. Each individual gene is a complex molecular factory built of deoxyribonucleic acids (DNA), ribonucleic acids (RNA), and proteins. All the physical characteristics of the resulting baby are determined by the genes. Eye color, tooth structure, basic metabolic rate, chemical balance, size of brain, shape of nose—everything is controlled by the genes in the zygote.

Lou's work seemed simple and straightforward to him. He was training Ramo, the computer, to look over the detailed structure of each gene in a zygote and compare it to the structure of a healthy, undamaged gene.

Ramo, being a computer, knew only what his human

co-workers told him. But he had two advantages that no human possessed. First, he had absolutely perfect memory. Once the "map" of a healthy gene was stored in the microcosmic magnetic patterns of his memory bank, he would never forget it, never blur or warp it, never let any emotional conditions prevent him from seeing it exactly as it was given to him. Second, Ramo could work at the speed of light, rather than the tediously slower pace of the human nervous system. Ramo could scan dozens of genes and spot the imperfections in their molecular structure in the time it took Lou to count to ten.

Lou often thought of himself as a teacher. His job was to teach an extremely clever youngster—Ramo—how to do a very complicated job. A job that no human could do because it would take him too long, and his memory wasn't good enough. Just before the Institute had been closed, Lou had taught Ramo all the patterns of healthy gene structures. Ramo knew what healthy genes looked like on a molecular level. Now Lou had to teach him how to compare a real set of genes with the healthy structures he already knew, how to spot the things that might be wrong with real genes, and how to show these imperfections in his viewscreens. Once this was done, Lou would begin to teach Ramo the biochemists' remedies for fixing faulty genes. And once *that* was done, the immense task was finished. The work of genetic engineering could begin.

But, sitting at the master control desk of the computer, Lou was much less than happy. The desk was a huge collection of control panels and viewscreens that reached around his padded chair in a semicircle. Within the reach of his fingers were controls that touched every part of Ramo's enormous electronic mind.

Lou was frowning as he slouched in the chair. He could see his own reflection in one of the dead viewscreens. He looked the way he felt. It was mid-morning, according to the clock, but here inside the computer building it was hard to tell. There were no windows. The building was frigidly air conditioned and heavily sound-proofed. Time meant very little to the computer.

Two weeks had gone by since Lou had come to the island. Two weeks, and Bonnie was still as cold and distant as she had been that first day. She worked for Lou, she did her job well. She had lunch with him most days and dinner a few times, in the tiny overcrowded cafeteria that Marcus had put up near the lab complex. She even mended a hole in his pants pocket. But she still acted more like a wary employee than a friend.

I should have never made them bring her here, Lou told himself for the millionth time that morning. *She'll never forgive me for it.*

The phone beside him buzzed. He punched the ANSWER button. Marcus' untanned, bland-looking face appeared on the main viewscreen.

"You wanted to see me?" he asked.

Nodding, Lou said, "Some of the biochemists have been asking me to help them program Ramo to handle their work. I don't mind helping them, but it's going to take time, and I thought you wanted me to plug ahead on the basic genetic mapping as fast as I can."

"The biochemists?" Marcus put on a worried frown. "Why do they need special computer programming?"

"They're working on something to do with drugs that affect the chemistry in the chromosomes, or something like . . ."

Marcus' eyes widened for a flash of a second. Then, he quickly regained his self-control. "No, you're quite right. You shouldn't be pulled off what you're doing to help with that. Let some of the other programmers help them."

Lou said, "Okay, fine . . . I'd be glad to help them if they need it."

"No," Marcus snapped. "Um, that is, they shouldn't interfere with your work in any way. I'll take care of it. If they come to you again, tell them to see me."

"Okay. Thanks."

Marcus nodded and cut off the connection. The viewscreen went blank, leaving Lou to look at his own frowning reflection again.

He worked at the control desk the rest of the morning, then around noontime phoned Bonnie. She was working with a trio of Chinese girls on the other side of the building.

"I'm afraid I can't go to lunch with you, Lou," she said without smiling. "The girls and I are eating right here at our desks; we've got mountains of work to do."

Lou punched the OFF button, and this time turned his gaze away from the viewscreen.

It was well past six o'clock when the phone buzzed again. It pulled Lou out of his total immersion in the work of teaching genetics to Ramo. He suddenly realized that he was bone tired: his back ached, his head was throbbing, his eyes burned. But on the main viewscreen

Ramo was displaying a detailed enlarged map of the molecular structure of a single gene. And part of the map —the area of the gene that was flawed—was outlined in red.

Lou typed on the master input keyboard, GOOD WORK RAMO. PERFECT. He muttered the words to himself as the phone kept on buzzing.

THANK YOU, Ramo flashed on the viewscreen.

Lou reached out and touched the phone button. Ramo's words disappeared from the screen and Anton Kori's lean angular face took form on it. He was grinning hugely, showing big white teeth with spaces between them that made them look like a cemetery to Lou.

"Can you have dinner with me?" Kori asked. "I have a lot to talk about, a lot to show you."

"Well, I don't know," Lou said. "I'm kind of beat. . . ."

"Oh." Kori's smile faded, but only a little. "Maybe Bonnie can . . . you have no objection? I've got to show these pictures to someone!"

"Bonnie?" Lou felt his nerves flash a warning. "Um . . . look, Anton—I'll give Bonnie a call and we'll both drop over to your place. Okay?"

Kori bobbed his head up and down. "Wonderful. Come to my lab. Next to the instrument repair shop. Bonnie knows where it is."

I've got no right to be sore at her, Lou told himself as he angrily punched out Bonnie's phone number. She wasn't in her room. Glancing at the clock, Lou tried her office phone.

Her face filled the screen and his anger melted.

"Oh, hello, Lou. I was just leaving for dinner."

Keeping his voice flat calm, "Kori just called. He's very excited about something, wants us to eat with him. Can you make it?"

"Sure." Without a moment's hesitation.

Lou asked, "Would you have been so free if I had asked you to have dinner with me? Alone?"

For an instant a frightened look flickered in her green eyes. "What do you mean, Lou?"

"You've been seeing a lot of Kori, haven't you?"

"Lou, I'm a tax-paying citizen . . . or at least I was until I got hijacked here. . . ."

"So you *are* sore about my having you brought here!"

"Of course I'm sore!" she flashed back. "Weren't you sore when they dragged you away? Do you enjoy being an exile? Is this island any better than the satellite or wherever it is that the rest of the Institute people were sent?"

Lou heard himself mumble, "You don't want to be around me, is that it?"

"Don't be sullen," she said, smiling for the first time. "Lou . . . whatever we had going between us back at the Institute, it can't be the same here. It just can't be."

"That's the way you want it?"

She looked sad and lonely now. "That's the way it's got to be, Lou."

"Yeah." He took a deep breath. "Well, how about dinner? I told Kori we'd both be over. . . ."

"All right," she said softly. "As long as we understand each other."

He nodded, his face frozen into a bitter mask. "I understand."

He left his office, walked around the computer building, and picked up Bonnie. They walked across the lab complex in silence. Overhead the trees filtered an unbelievable sunset sky of pink and saffron and soft violet. Through the boles of the trees, off at the edge of the reddened sea, the sun was huge and distended as it touched the horizon.

If Bonnie and Lou had little to say to each other, Anton Kori more than filled their silence. The moment they stepped through the door into his cluttered laboratory/workroom, he started chattering.

"It's fantastic, you'll never believe it, it's like something out of the cinema. . . ."

He bustled around the big room, dragging a table loaded with complex electronic gear across the floor and positioning it near the door.

"Lou, would you turn on the switch for the laser?" Kori pointed to the wall over his workbench. "No, not that one! The next one, on your left. Yes."

Lou flicked the switch. He saw nothing in the room that looked like a laser, but there was a hum of electrical power coming from someplace.

"Wait 'til you see this . . . Bonnie, the lights, please. Behind you."

With a slightly amused smile, Bonnie turned off the overhead lights. In the darkened room, Kori's bony face was eerily lit by the glow of the equipment on his table.

"Now just a minute while I use this old slide for focusing. . . ." he muttered.

Lou found a rolling chair and pushed it over toward Bonnie. She sat, and he stood beside her, facing the slightly luminescent viewscreen at the far end of the room. A slide came on, some sort of graph, with many colored curves weaving across it.

"Now the focus," Kori mumbled. The graph suddenly became three-dimensional. The curves seemed to stand in the middle of the room. Lou felt he could walk around them and look at them from the other side.

"Okay, good." Kori said, so excited that his English had a decided Slavic edge to it. "Now we see what no man has ever seen before—except me."

The room went totally dark for an instant, and then it was filled with stars. Lou heard Bonnie gasp. It was like being out in space, stars as far as the eye could see: white, yellow, orange, red, blue—unblinking points of fire in the black depths of space. In the distance, the nebulous haze of the Milky Way glowed softly.

"Wide angle view, looking aft," Kori explained matter-of-factly. "That bright yellow star in the center is—the sun."

"These are the tapes from the *Starfarer*?" Lou asked, and immediately felt sheepish because it was such a needless question.

He sensed Kori nodding in the darkness. "It took the ship more than thirty years to reach the vicinity of Alpha Centauri. And it took more than four years just for the laser beam to carry this information back to us."

Another moment of darkness and then another picture of stars.

"Wide view forward," Kori said.

There was still a bright yellow star in the center of the field of view. Kori flicked through several more holograms. The yellow star grew brighter, closer. Soon, Lou could see that it was two stars.

"Alpha Centauri," Kori said in an awed voice, as if anything louder might shatter the pictures. "Proxima is so distant and faint from its two big brothers that I haven't been able to pinpoint it yet. It's out among those background stars someplace. We need an astronomer here!"

Lou shared Kori's awe. "Alpha Centauri," he echoed.

"You were right, Anton," said Bonnie. "This is fantastic . . . so beautiful."

"Wait," Kori answered. "You haven't seen the best yet."

He flicked through another dozen holograms. The double star grew larger. Lou could see that one of the stars was smaller and redder than the big yellow sun.

"What are those two flecks, near the yellow star?" Lou asked

Kori giggled excitedly. "Flecks? Flecks indeed! Those are planets! Two planets orbiting around Alpha Centauri!"

Lou had no words. He simply stared at the screen as Kori flicked on several more holograms, closer and closer, of the two worlds. On the very last slide only the second-most planet was in view. It looked like a fat round ball, yellowish-green, streaked with white clouds.

"I haven't had a chance to analyze the spectroscopic data," Kori said, "but those clouds look like water vapor to me. It's a bigger planet than Earth, probably a heavier gravity. But if there's water, there could be life!"

It was very late when Bonnie and Lou walked with Kori back to the dormitory. None of them had eaten dinner. In their excitement over the star pictures they had simply forgotten all about it.

Kori stopped in the middle of the road, at a spot where the trees didn't overhang, and threw his head back.

"Look at them!" he shouted. "Millions and billions of stars. And millions and billions of planets. Some of them must be just like this Earth, waiting for us to reach them. And we can! We can reach them, and we will!" He laughed loudly, and then gave a shattering shrill whistle as he swung his long arms up toward the sky.

"Hey, easy . . . you sound like you're high," Lou said.

"I *am* high," Kori answered happily. "I'm drunk with joy and knowledge and power. We can reach out to new Earths. That's enough to make any man drunk."

Lou shook his head in the moonless dark. "Maybe we'll need new Earths. We've certainly fouled up this one."

Kori laughed. He wasn't in the mood for seriousness. "Wait until the people of the world see these pictures. Wait until they realize what it means. . . ."

"I thought the government wasn't going to let the news out," Bonnie said.

Lou answered, "Marcus and Minister Bernard will get the pictures out to the newsmen somehow, I'll bet."

Her voice was quiet but firm. "Will they? Do you really think that they intend to let the world know about this? Or about genetic engineering, when we get it to work right?"

Lou stopped and looked at her. In the darkness, he couldn't see the expression on her face.

"What are you saying?" he asked.

For a moment Bonnie didn't reply. Then, "I'm not sure . . . I could be wrong. There's nothing definite, but I've just got a . . . well, a feeling, sort of . . ."

"Go on."

"Well . . . why do they have Anton working on nuclear explosives? What guarantees do we have that our work will be made public? Why are the biochemists working on cortical suppressors. . . ?"

"Suppressors?"

"Uh-huh. I just found out this afternoon," Bonnie said. "That's what they need the computer time for: to select the chemical suppressor that does the best job of degrading cortical activity—permanently."

"But that would destroy a person's intelligence," Lou said.

"I know," Bonnie answered. "And I think they're planning to use Big George as a guinea pig."

Lou felt a hot bomb go off in his guts. "No, they wouldn't . . . if this is true, then . . ."

"Then we've been tricked into working for a group of people who're planning to overthrow the government and turn half the world's people into mindless zombies," Bonnie said.

There was a long, long silence, broken only by the night sounds of insects from the trees and brush, and the distant sigh of the surf. Finally, Kori's voice floated ruefully through the darkness:

"Well, at least I don't feel drunk anymore."

Chapter 14

It took Lou nearly a week to convince himself that Bonnie was right.

He used Ramo as his source of information and his teacher. He didn't know very much about the work the biochemists were doing. So he followed their progress by checking Ramo's programs and memory bank every evening, after his own work was finished. Within his vast memory Ramo stored most of the world's knowledge of biochemistry. So the computer became Lou's teacher, and explained patiently and with machinelike thoroughness exactly what Marcus' biochemists were trying to do.

By the end of the week Lou knew enough.

He sat on the warm beach sand, Bonnie on one side of him and Kori on the other. About two dozen people, most of them men and women from the technical staff, were on the beach or swimming in the gentle surf that rolled in from the reef. Far off on the horizon, huge towering cumulus clouds paraded like happy children across the sky.

The three of them sat a little bit away from all the rest of the bathers. Bonnie was still wet from a brief swim. Her skin was glistening with droplets of water, and prickled from chill. Or was it fear, in this warm afternoon? In the back of his mind, Lou noted with appreciation that there was plenty of her skin to be seen with the brief swimsuit she was wearing.

But he kept his face serious and his voice low enough so that it could just be heard by the two of them over the shouting and laughter of the others on the beach.

"You were entirely right, Bonnie," Lou said. "The biochemists are working on suppressors. They've already produced test samples of a drug and they've injected it into mice. Ramo showed me the test results. Six mice starved to death in mazes because they couldn't find their way to the food at the end of the maze. Before they had been injected, the same mice had made it through the same mazes in less than a minute."

"Oh my God," Kori said. Bonnie shivered.

Lou went on grimly. "And today they asked Ramo for the complete cortical layout on Big George. There's no doubt about it . . . they're going to try the drug on him."

"And then on a human being," Bonnie said.

Lou glanced up at her face. Then he nodded. "Yeah, you're right. That would be the next step."

"What do we do?" Kori wondered aloud.

Lou shrugged. "There are only two things I can think of. First, we can stop the work we're doing . . . just refuse to do any more. That would slow them down on their genetic engineering and their nuclear bombs. . . ."

"But it wouldn't stop this suppressor business at all," Bonnie pointed out.

"And they already have enough bombs to destroy Messina, if they want to," Kori said.

Lou nodded and traced a square in the sand with his

finger. "Okay . . . then the only other thing we can do is wipe out Ramo."

"Blow up the computer?" Kori asked.

"No . . . I can just erase all his programs and memory banks. Take a little time and some tinkering, but I could do it."

"It would take more than a little time," Bonnie said. "Ramo's banks . . ."

"I know a few tricks I haven't shown you," Lou said grinning. "I could wipe Ramo clean in a night."

"Really? That would stop everything they're doing," Kori said.

"They'd still have the bombs," Lou countered.

Shrugging, Kori said, "Yes, but without the biological weapons they're trying to get, the bombs by themselves wouldn't be enough for them."

Bonnie shook her head. "You're forgetting something else that they'd still have."

"What?"

"Us . . . or really you, Lou. If Ramo is wiped clean, don't you think Marcus is smart enough to figure out who did it?"

"Okay," Lou said evenly. "So he'll know I did it. What good does that do him? Ramo will still be blanked out. Marcus will be stopped dead."

"And so will you be," Bonnie said. "He'll kill you."

"That wouldn't do him any good."

"It wouldn't do *you* any good, either," said Kori.

"Don't you see?" Bonnie said. "Killing you doesn't help him, I admit. But the threat of killing you will stop you from erasing Ramo."

Lou nodded. "It does take a lot of the fun out of the idea."

Kori said, "Wait . . . we've left something out of the equation. We're all assuming that we must stay on this island. . . ."

"You know a way off?" Lou asked.

"Well, there are boats every few days. . . ."

"Can you sail one? Can the three of us take over one of the boats? Can you navigate? Do any of us even know where on Earth this island is?"

Dismal silence.

Then Kori brightened again. "If we can't get off the island, maybe we can signal someone to bring government troops here to rescue us!"

In spite of himself, Lou laughed out loud. "Okay, great idea. How are you going to signal? And who do you signal?"

Frowning in puzzlement, Kori mumbled, "Well . . . there's a radio station down by the harbor."

"Yeah, and three armed guards at the door all the time. And even if we could get in and operate the radio, and make contact with somebody, we'd be dead before any government people got to this island."

Kori clasped his hands behind his head and stretched out on the sand. "Louis, my friend, I am a physicist, I have come up with a great basic idea. I admit that there are a few details to be ironed out. That's the work of engineers, not physicists." He closed his eyes and pretended to go to sleep.

Without a word, Bonnie picked up a fistful of sand and

dumped it on Kori's face. He sputtered and sat up. They all laughed together.

Bonnie stood up. "Come on, let's take a dip before dinner. We're not going to solve the problem right now."

Lou got up beside her. "Maybe not. But we'd better solve it pretty fast. We don't have much time left."

Lou couldn't sleep that night. He lay in his narrow bed, peering into the darkness, listening to the night sounds outside. The room's only window was open to the sea breeze. A million thoughts kept crowding in on him. No matter how he turned or punched the pillow or forced his eyes shut or tried to relax, he still found himself lying in the rumpled bed, sticky with perspiration, his eyes open and jaw clenched achingly tight with tension.

Finally he admitted defeat, got up and dressed. He walked out into the darkness, down the road toward the laboratory buildings. And the computer.

He turned around the corner of the first lab building and went toward the fence of Big George's compound. Down the way he could see a guard sitting by the gate, drowsing. The moon was riding in and out of scudding silvery clouds, but inside the compound the shadows cast by the trees made everything dark. Straining his eyes, Lou thought he saw the bulky shape of the gorilla sleeping on a man-made pallet of wood, straw, and palm fronds. Then he heard a snuffle and the big dark shape moved sluggishly.

"It's okay," Lou called softly. "It's me, Georgy."

The gorilla sat up and Lou could see a glint of moonlight reflected off his eyes. Big George pulled himself off the pallet and shuffled over to the fence.

"Uncle Lou," he whispered.

"How are you, Georgy?"

"Good. I been very good."

Lou wanted to reach out and pat him, but the wire fence was too fine a mesh to allow his hand through.

"I know you've been good, Georgy. Do you like it here? Has everybody been nice to you?"

"I have lots of room to play and they feed me good. But nobody comes to play with me. I'm all alone."

"I'm sorry . . . I haven't been to see you as much as I should," Lou replied guiltily.

"But the doctor said he'd come and play with me," George whispered.

"The doctor? What doctor?"

"The doctor," George answered. "He was here today . . . or was it yesterday? Do you call it today if it was the day before tonight?"

"Never mind," Lou said impatiently. "What doctor? Who was he?"

"He's a new friend. He said he's going to play with me when he comes back again. And I didn't move or yell or do anything, even when it hurt."

"What did he do to you?"

The gorilla touched the back of his head with a huge clumsy hand. "He made a funny noise back here, and it hurt a little. But just a little. It feels all better now."

Spinal tap, Lou thought, his innards sinking.

"I promised I wouldn't move even if it hurt," George said.

"Georgy, listen. The doctor . . . he said he'd be back. When? When's he coming back?"

"Tomorrow."

Tomorrow. This morning, most likely. "Okay, Georgy, you get back to sleep now. I'll come and see you tomorrow."

"All right, Uncle Lou. Good night."

"Good night."

As the gorilla shambled back toward his pallet, Lou began to know what real responsibility felt like. *Big George trusts me,* he told himself. *He needs me to keep them from hurting him.*

And then with a shock Lou realized that the only way he could save Big George would be to destroy Ramo. He almost laughed as he stood by the wire fence in the moonlight.

Some family I've got, he thought bitterly. *A gorilla and a computer. One of them is going to die. And it's up to me to choose which one.*

He hesitated only for a moment. Then he turned and headed for the computer building.

Chapter 15

The door to the computer building was locked. Not by a voice-code lock, but an old-fashioned mechanical type, the kind that has a set of nine buttons that must be pushed in the right combination.

Lou didn't know the combination. *And I'll bet Marcus has the building wired with alarms. There'd be guards swarming in here before I sat down in the control slot.*

He stood there for a moment, uncertain. *No sense getting shot if you can't do the job you set out to do,* he told himself. And then he smiled. *On the other hand, if you're smart enough, and quick enough, there might be a way to get the job done without killing anybody.*

Grinning with his new idea, Lou walked back to the dormitory, undressed quickly, and got into bed. He set his wristwatch alarm to buzz at six, then closed his eyes. In five minutes he was sound asleep.

He had less than three hours of sleep, but Lou felt bright and ready as he stood by the fence of George's compound again.

"Here's some fruit I saved from breakfast," he said to the gorilla. "Catch!"

He tossed a banana and two oranges over the fence. George backpedaled clumsily and managed to grab the banana in one huge hand. The oranges fell to the ground.

He stooped to pick them up, then jammed all three into his mouth.

"Thank you, Uncle Lou," Big George said juicily.

Lou laughed. "You're welcome, Georgy."

Out of the corner of his eye, Lou saw a guard walking past the lab buildings, stopping at each door briefly to touch out a combination on the lock. He talked with the gorilla for a few minutes more, then, when he was sure that the guard was out of sight, Lou walked briskly to the computer building.

The rest of the technical staff was probably just getting up, Lou thought as he glanced at the control panel clock. Sliding into the seat, he immediately started typing out instructions for Ramo.

It was mid-morning before he found out if his scheme had worked. Despite the computer room's nearly arctic air conditioning, Lou was sweating as he sat at the control desk. He was trying to do his own work, but it was going very slowly. His mind certainly wasn't on it.

The phone buzzed. Lou was expecting it, but it still made him jump. He touched the ANSWER button. The round Oriental face of the chief biochemist appeared on the screen. He looked unhappy.

"We seem to have a problem this morning," he said without preamble.

"Really?" Lou said as innocently as he could.

Still frowning, the biochemist said, "Yes. We went to run a routine check of yesterday's work and found that the data we recorded yesterday is missing from the computer's memory bank."

"Missing?" Lou shook his head. "Impossible. You're probably just searching the wrong bank."

They talked it over for nearly half an hour. The results of yesterday's spinal tap on the gorilla, the cortical map, even some of the chemical formulas that had been stored in the computer weeks earlier—all were gone from Ramo's memory banks.

Lou forced himself to look serious. "I'll do a complete check to find the missing data," he said, "but it sounds to me like some of your people have goofed up. Running this computer isn't as simple as operating a typewriter, you know. You should have let me record your data . . . or at least you ought to have a trained computer programmer or technician doing the job."

"They are trained technicians!" the biochemist snapped.

Lou shrugged. "Then they haven't been trained well enough. . . . Okay, I'll look for the data for you. But I'm willing to bet it was never stored properly in the first place, and it's simply not in the memory banks."

The biochemist was starting to look furious. "Two months of work lost!" He lapsed into Chinese.

It took them a week to figure out what was going on. Lou would spend his days at his own work, and then at the end of the day he'd have Ramo review the biochemists' work for him. It took him only a few minutes to erase some of their material from Ramo's memory banks. Lou never washed out very much material, just enough to slow them down.

The biochemists became a very unhappy group of people. Their chief went around screaming and purple-faced. The computer technicians who worked for them looked scared. By the end of the week, Lou was spending most of his day with the technicians, trying to find out why they couldn't do their jobs properly.

Lou told nobody what he was doing. But Bonnie and Kori guessed it. By the end of the week, at dinner with them in the noisy cafeteria, Lou said to Kori:

"You've got to figure out some way to get us off this island. It's only a matter of time until the biochemists figure out what's wrong with their computer programs, and then . . ."

"I know," Kori answered, hunching over the table and speaking as low as possible, "I've been trying to work out a navigational fix, so that we can at least find out where we are. But I'm afraid I'm not much of a navigator. And the sextant I've built isn't very accurate."

"But how do we get off the island?" Bonnie asked.

Kori shrugged. "Maybe we could build a raft. . . ."

"Or a flying carpet," Lou replied acidly.

That ended their discussion.

It happened the next day. Lou wasn't really surprised when an armed guard showed up at the computer control room. It had been exactly a week since he had first started tinkering with Ramo's biochemistry banks.

"What is it?" Lou asked, tensing.

The guard said, with a Malay lilt to this voice, "Mr. Marcus wishes to see you."

"I'm busy at the moment. Tell him . . ."

"Now," the guard said. And he hitched a thumb on the holster at his hip.

Lou nodded. "Okay, just let me . . ."

"Do not touch the computer controls," the guard said

softly, even gently. But his hand curled around the butt of his gun.

Lou found that his own hands were suddenly trembling, and well away from the controls. "Okay, okay, but the computer's in the middle of a run."

"Some other technicians are being brought in to take care of it. You will come with me, please."

Marcus' car was waiting outside, with another guard at the wheel. Lou climbed in and the first guard sat beside him. In a few minutes, Lou was ushered into the air-conditioned study of Marcus' house. It was a small room, lined with books and a single large window that overlooked the sea.

Marcus was sitting at a desk in front of the window. There were a few straight-backed chairs in the room, and a comfortable-looking sofa. Marcus was talking into the viewphone on his desk when Lou entered. Without looking up, he gestured Lou to a chair next to the desk.

If he was angry, he wasn't showing it. His face had its normal calm expression as he said quietly to the phone screen, "We've tracked down the source of the trouble and we'll get things back under control and on schedule."

Lou couldn't see the screen, but heard the voice reply, "Very well. See that you do. The timing is very critical."

"I understand. Good-by."

"Good-by."

Marcus pressed the OFF button, stared into the screen for a few moments longer, then turned to face Lou.

"You surprise me," he said.

"I do?"

Marcus almost smiled. "Let's not play games, Christopher. You've been sabotaging our computer programs, slowing down our biochemistry project. Why?"

"How do you know it's me?" Lou stalled.

"It's fairly obvious," Marcus leaned forward in his chair slightly. "Now listen, Christopher. You're not in the States any more. You're playing in a different league, with different rules. I don't have to prove it's you who's screwing up the computer. I think it's you, and I'm going ahead on that assumption. I called you here to find out why you're doing it, and to tell you what's going to happen if you don't stop."

Lou felt anger rising up inside him. "Just like that, huh? Somebody's messing up the computer and I get blamed. What happens now, do you shoot me?"

"No, nothing so dramatic," Marcus answered. In a voice that sounded genuinely concerned, he said, "You know, I really think you're more worried about that gorilla than about your own skin."

"Yeah. I'm a gorilla freak."

Shaking his head like a patient father, Marcus said, "All right, play it tough if you want to. But listen to this, and get it straight. We're going to overthrow the world government. Never mind who 'we' consists of. There are some very important people in our group. We're playing for the highest stakes there are, and we don't intend to let you or anyone else stand in our way."

"Is that why you've got Kori making bombs?"

"Of course. Did you ever hear of a government that allowed itself to be pushed out of power without a fight?

We're developing three weapons here on this island: nuclear bombs, the cortical suppressor, and genetic engineering."

Lou said, "So you can blow up your enemies, turn the survivors into morons, and then—after you've taken over —you can control everyone's children."

"That's not one hundred percent right, but it's pretty close."

"It doesn't sound like a very happy world that you're aiming to set up."

"Oh no? And what kind of a world do we have now? The government's letting the cities fester worse and worse, more and more barbarians being born and pushing out into the civilized parts of the world. How long do you think it'll be before we see something like a plague of rats sweeping across the whole world? Two-legged rats, from New York and Rio and Tokyo and Calcutta and Rome . . . every big city in the world!"

"And your answer is to bomb them out or turn them into zombies."

"If we have to," Marcus said, in the same tone he would use to offer a drink. "The bombs are really for fighting the government troops. Once we've taken over, we'll have other means of handling the barbarians— including the suppressors."

Lou shook his head.

"I wish I could get through to you," Marcus insisted. "What's this government done for you? Put you in exile, you and all your friends. When we take over, you can go back to living normal, useful lives."

"Useful to whom?"

With great earnestness, Marcus said, "Listen to reason, will you? You and the other scientists will be among the top people in the new society. Your children will get the best genetic care that you yourselves can provide."

"Until somebody decides he doesn't like what we're doing, or what we're thinking," Lou answered. "This government's slapped us in exile—*your* friends might not be so lenient."

Marcus sank back in his chair, as if baffled. "I don't have the time to argue with you. We're going ahead, and there's nothing you can do to stop us. If you don't stop tinkering with our biochemistry project, you're going to get hurt."

"No I'm not," Lou flashed back. "You need me to make the genetic engineering a success, remember? And that's where the real jackpot is. Because you might be able to surprise the government and knock it off, you might be able to take over the whole world . . . but without genetic engineering, you'll never be able to *control* the world. I'm beginning to see how your minds work, and I know why genetic engineering is so important to you. You want to control everybody, don't you? Make your own children supermen, and everybody else's their slaves. Right?"

Marcus shook his head. "Not exactly. You make it sound . . ."

"Rotten. Filthy and rotten. And that's what it is. But you need it, and that means you need me. I'm the key man, you told me so yourself."

"There are others. . . ."

"Then why'd you yank me out of exile? Because it'd take anybody else at least a year to catch up to where I am. I understand the whole genetic engineering problem, and there's plenty of it tucked away in my head, not in any computer banks or notebooks. So don't try to threaten me, unless you want to wait a year or more for the ability to control the next generation of children."

Marcus leaned back in his chair with a more-in-sorrow-than-anger look on his bland face. Shaking his head wearily, he said, "You still don't realize what you're up against, do you? Why do you think we went to the trouble of finding that blonde girl friend of yours and bringing her here? We don't have to threaten you. If you're worried about what we're going to do to your precious gorilla, try to imagine what could happen to the girl. Things could get very unpleasant for her. Very unpleasant."

Lou gripped the arms of his chair hard enough to make his hands hurt. He was fighting an instinct to spring at Marcus and smash his bland, evil face.

"Just try to control yourself and do as you're told," Marcus went on. "If you can behave, everything will be fine for you. But if you keep working against me . . . the girl will suffer for it."

"If you hurt her I'll kill you." Lou was almost surprised to hear himself say it, to hear the cold flat metallic ring of his own voice.

Marcus' expression didn't change. "Christopher, we shouldn't be threatening each other. Just do your work and neither you nor anyone else will get hurt. That's all we're asking from you. As for the gorilla, it'll probably be happier at its natural intelligence level than it is now."

The greatest excuse in the world, Lou thought. *They'll*

be happier doing what I want them to do instead of what they themselves want to do.

Without saying another word, Lou got up and started for the door.

"Wait a minute," Marcus called. "You haven't said . . ."

Lou turned. "You've got all the answers you need. There's no way for me to stop you."

Trembling with rage, he left the office, walked past the guard lounging outside the door, went out of the house, ignored the car still parked in front with its driver, and walked back toward the dormitory.

As he passed the lab complex, Kori came running up to him.

"Lou, I've been looking for you everywhere!"

Lou didn't answer.

"I've figured it out!" Kori whispered excitedly as he pulled up beside Lou. "How to get the government troops here. And quickly! Inside of a few days!"

Lou shook his head. "It'll be too late."

Chapter 16

Kori grabbed his arm and stopped him. "No, I'm serious. We can do it!"

Lou said, "In a few days they'll have ruined Big George, maybe killed him. And if we try to stop them, they'll take it out on Bonnie."

"What?"

"That's what Marcus just told me. If he doesn't like the way we behave, Bonnie'll suffer for it."

"But he can't . . ."

"Yes he can. And he will. I bet he'd even enjoy it."

Kori's face turned as red as the setting sun. "That pudding-faced pipsqueak. I'll . . ."

Now Lou took Kori's arm. "Hold on. There's nothing we can do about it."

He felt Kori's surge of anger fade away, saw his face return to normal, except for a sullen smoldering in his eyes.

"What do we do now?" Kori asked.

"I don't know," said Lou. "What was your scheme all about? How can you signal for government troops?"

"Oh that. . . . With the navigation satellites."

"Navigation satellites? How . . ."

"They have sensors on them to detect nuclear explosions."

"They what?"

Kori started walking toward the dorm again, and Lou trudged along beside him. "It's a holdover from the old days, before the world government disarmed all the nations," Kori explained. "All the navigation satellites have a special array of sensors to watch out for nuclear explosions. If anybody sets off a bomb on the Earth's surface, in the atmosphere, or even in space, the government is alerted instantly. Inside of a few hours, there's an inspection team at the site of the explosion to find out what's going on. An *armed* inspection team. With troops ready to follow at an instant's notice."

"But nobody's set off a bomb for . . ."

"I know, but the government still has the teams, and they even hold practice drills. I was an advisor to a group of new recruits two years ago."

Lou chuckled. "I guess once a government agency gets a job to do, they keep on doing it, whether it's needed or not."

"Don't complain," Kori said. "Now then, the bombs I've been making are stored in caves at the far end of the island. If one of them went off, and a satellite spotted the blast, there would be an inspection team here in a matter of hours."

"Can you set them off?"

"Them?" Kori laughed. "One will be enough. If they all go off, they'll wipe out this entire island. Do you know how much destructive force even a single kiloton contains?"

When they got to the dormitory, Lou sent Kori up to get Bonnie. He didn't want to talk inside of any building.

Too easy to plant electronic bugs indoors. As he stood by the dormitory entrance, Lou got the feeling he was being watched. *Nerves,* he told himself. But he knew that if he were in Marcus' place, he'd have guards out watching the troublemakers. *And we're going to make enough trouble to slide this island into the sea, if we have to,* Lou thought unsmilingly.

They ate a quick dinner in the cafeteria and then walked out to the beach. Walking ankle-deep through the warm-lapping waves, with the surf booming on the reef a kilometer out, they talked over their plans as the dying red sun stretched their shadows fantastically before them.

"I'll need at least two days to round up the proper equipment," Kori was saying.

"Make it one day," Lou answered over the roar of the surf. "Big George doesn't have two days to spare."

Kori glanced at Bonnie, then looked at Lou. "We want to do this right. If we rush, something might . . ."

"One day," Lou said flatly.

Shrugging, Kori agreed. "All right. One day."

"Where can we plant the bomb without setting off all the others?" Bonnie asked.

"That's why I wanted the extra day," Kori said, "to find the best location. Probably the best thing to do is to bury it in the beach sand across the island from the storage caves. That ought to be safe enough."

"Will it make a big enough explosion for a satellite to see if you bury it?" Lou asked.

Kori laughed. "Have no fear. A few feet of sand isn't going to smother one of my toys."

"Okay."

"I'll need two things," Kori said, more seriously. "A car to carry equipment and everything, and a diversion so I can get into the storage caves and do what I must do without being stopped by the guards."

"What about the guards at the caves?" Lou asked.

"There's usually only one. I think I can handle him easily enough."

"You're sure?"

Kori drew himself up to full height. He towered several inches over Lou, but he still looked spindly. "My friend, I was a national fencing champion five years ago. I still keep in good shape. Besides that, I'm sneaky. I'll ask the guard to help me carry some of the equipment and then hit him when his hands are full and his back turned."

Laughing, Bonnie said, "My hero."

"Never mind," Lou said. "Heroics are exactly what we don't need. We need good, sneaky, practical action that works. I don't want to win any moral victory; we'll all end up dead that way."

Kori nodded.

"Okay," Lou continued, "so you need a car and a diversion. We'll figure that out, shouldn't be too tough a problem. But the big question is, how do we protect Bonnie?"

"She's got to disappear," Kori said.

"Great. How do we do it?"

Silence.

They walked slowly under the purpling sky. A surge of sea curled around their ankles, then ebbed away. A lone gull glided low over the waves, calling sadly as if looking for long-vanished friends.

Finally Bonnie said, "Big George! I could stay in his

compound for a day or so. There are plenty of trees and bushes to hide in and the guards never go in there."

"With the gorilla?" It was too dark to see Kori's face, but his voice sounded aghast.

"We're friends," Bonnie said. "We've known each other since George was born."

"He wouldn't hurt her," Lou agreed. "Or anybody else, for that matter. Trouble is, he'd want you to play with him. You wouldn't be able to stay hidden. He'd give you away."

"No, not if I explained it to him."

Kori shook his head. "I know you think a lot of that animal, and his intelligence has been boosted. But I wouldn't plan to stay inside that fence with him for ten minutes, let alone twelve hours or more."

"Oh, you've seen too many movies," Bonnie said. "George wouldn't hurt anybody."

They went on talking, planning, arguing until it was completely dark. The stars filled the night and the shimmering band of the Milky Way arched across the sky, bright and beckoning.

"Look up there!" Kori said.

In the darkness they could see his shadowy outline pointing skyward. Looking up, Lou saw one star moving silently, purposefully through the heavens, as if it had detached itself from its normal position to carry out some mission.

"Is that one of the satellites?" Bonnie's voice floated through the dark against the *basso* background of the surf.

Kori glanced at his luminescent wristwatch. "Yes. And right on schedule."

"Thank God," said Lou.

Lou didn't sleep much that night, and the next day at the computer building he hardly paid any attention to his work. He went through the motions, but his mind was racing, thinking about all that had to be done that night. Get the car for Kori, get Bonnie into hiding, create a diversion that will draw off the guards long enough for Kori to work unnoticed.

Toward the end of the afternoon, Lou couldn't stay cooped up in the control room any longer. He stepped outside and took a deep breath of warm, salt-smelling air.

Then the quiet afternoon was shattered by the tortured scream of an animal. A scream of rage and pain and fear.

"George!"

Chapter 17

Lou ran to the gorilla's compound. He got there in time to see two of the biochemists carrying a third through the gate. Big George was nowhere in sight. A half-dozen guards were clustered around the gate and more were arriving on the run, guns drawn.

"What happened?" Lou shouted.

They ignored him. A pair of guards took the unconscious biochemist from his co-workers. His face was bloody and one arm was hanging at a weird angle.

Lou grabbed one of the sweating biochemists.

"What happened? What did you do?"

The little Oriental looked up at Lou with fear and anger in his eyes. In a nasal, heavily-accented English he said, "Ape got frightened by injections. Anesthetic wore off. Restraints not strong enough. Ape broke loose, knocked down Dr. Kusawa, ran back into trees."

"Injections?" Lou demanded. "The suppressors?"

The biochemist nodded, pulled his arm out of Lou's grasp, and tottered away, following the guards who were carrying his boss.

Lou went to the gate.

One of the guards started shaking his head and motioning Lou away. "No. Danger. Keep away."

"Let me in there. He won't hurt me. He's scared and hurt."

The guards were clustered around the gate, which was now firmly locked. Most of them were peering into the trees and brush. Big George was not in sight. The other guards were watching Lou.

"Danger," said the one guard to Lou. "Go away."

Slowly, reluctantly, Lou walked away.

At dinner that night, Kori shook his head. "That makes everything different. Bonnie can't stay in there with him now."

"Sure I can," Bonnie said. "George will be all right by now, and the guards will never dream of searching his compound. It's a better hiding place than ever, now."

"No," said Lou. "There's no way of telling what those injections did to him. It's too risky."

They sat at their table in the cafeteria, leaning forward in a tight little huddle, ignoring their cooling dinner trays, oblivious of the fact that many eyes were watching them in the busy, noisy cafeteria.

Bonnie insisted that George was all right. "Let's go down to his compound and talk to him. Then we'll see for sure," she suggested.

Lou nodded agreement. Kori simply looked worried.

They walked down to the gorilla's compound, but stayed away from the gate where the guards stood watch. They moved up onto the slope of the hill to a spot close to the trees inside the compound.

"Georgy," Lou called out softly. "Georgy, it's me, Uncle Lou."

A snuffling grunt, and from the shadows in among the

trees a pair of baleful eyes suddenly gleamed out at them. Despite himself, Lou shuddered. Those eyes were glaring like a jungle beast's.

He forced his voice to stay calm. "Georgy, it's all right. It's me, Uncle Lou. And Bonnie is here, too. And another friend. . . ."

A growl.

Lou turned to Kori. "Maybe it's a good idea for you to go away, Anton. George must be scared out of his wits of strangers right now."

"He doesn't sound scared."

"He is."

Stubbornly, Kori said, "But I want to see the gorilla's reactions for myself. I don't want you two making any mistakes about this. . . ."

"Shove it!" Lou snapped, keeping his voice down to avoid frightening Big George. "You think you're the only one with brains? I'm not going to let Bonnie take any chances."

"Stop arguing," Bonnie said. To Kori she added, "He won't come out as long as you're here."

Kori left, muttering to himself. After another ten minutes of coaxing and soothing, Big George lumbered out of the trees and up to the fence.

"Georgy," Lou said, gripping the fine wire mesh of the fence. "Are you okay?"

"Head . . . head hurts."

"It's all right, Georgy," Bonnie said. "The hurt will go away soon."

"Hurts . . . bad men . . . hurt . . ."

Is it just me or does his voice sound strange? Like it's

hard for him to put words together. Lou felt his eyes stinging and realized there were tears in them. "Georgy, don't be afraid. It's going to be all right. The bad men have gone away. They won't come back."

The gorilla merely blinked.

Bonnie said softly. "Georgy, in a little while I'm going to come and stay with you. I'll bring you lots of food, and some medicine to stop the hurt.

"Hurt . . . scared . . . bad men . . ."

"I'll stay with you," Bonnie repeated. "And the medicine will stop the hurting. Don't be afraid."

"And I'll make sure that the bad men don't ever come back," Lou said, feeling anger welling up within him. "Not ever."

"Uncle Lou . . ." Big George started, but his voice trailed off and he never finished the thought.

Lou said as gently as he could. "It's all right, Georgy. No one's ever going to hurt you again."

As they walked away from the compound, Bonnie put a hand on Lou's arm.

"You're shaking," she said.

Nodding, Lou answered, "You know . . . last night I couldn't sleep. I was scared. Still am, I guess. We could all get killed tonight. But I think what was really scaring me the most was the thought that I might have to kill somebody myself. Or at least try to. But now . . . seeing what they've done to Georgy . . . to a harmless animal like that . . . I'm not shaking from fear anymore. That's anger."

"It's all right," Bonnie said. "Everything's going to be fine."

"Do you really think you'll be okay in there with George?"

"Yes, of course. I'll bring him some candy and sedatives. He'll sleep like a baby."

Lou nodded.

"You'll see," Bonnie said. "It's all going to go like clockwork."

"Yeah." Lou glanced at his wristwatch. *X minus four hours and counting.*

Exactly at eleven o'clock the three of them met at the doorway to the dormitory building. They had spent the intervening hours checking final details and then pretending to go to their separate rooms for the night. Now they met in the darkness and started wordlessly for the lab complex. They had found identical black stretch pullovers and slacks among the disposable clothing supply in the dorm. *Identical, but Bonnie's sure looks better than ours,* Lou thought.

There were two cars on the island, turbowagons, both of them. One was usually parked for the night at the lab complex. The other stayed at Marcus' house.

"Do you think anybody's watching us?" Bonnie asked in a whisper as they walked along the side of the road toward the lab area, sticking to the shadows of the trees and shrubs.

Kori whispered back, "They've got guards posted at the lab complex, the gorilla's compound, the bomb storage caves, and Marcus' house. Why should they watch us? We can't do any harm unless we get to one or more of those spots."

"Well, if they are watching us we'll find out about it soon enough," Lou said, pointing to the glow up the road that marked the lights of the lab complex.

They skirted the lighted area by detouring through the trees, making a wide circle, and doubling back to the far side of Big George's compound. While Kori stayed well away, Lou and Bonnie walked up to the fence and softly called the gorilla.

Big George lumbered up to the fence. "Hello, Georgy," said Lou. "How do you feel?"

"Head . . . hurts . . ."

"I've brought some medicine to make it feel all better," Bonnie said. "And some candy for you."

They talked for a few moments more with the gorilla, then Lou boosted Bonnie up to the top of the wire fence. George reached up and grasped her around the waist, his huge hands circling her completely. He put her down inside the fence as gently as a ballet dancer handles his ballerina.

Lou watched them, his innards suddenly knotting as he realized how easily Big George could kill Bonnie. But she reached up and patted his massive head. They turned and went toward the trees together as Bonnie reached into the bag at her waist for some candy.

Despite his fears, Lou grinned at the slim blonde girl and the hulking gorilla. *If only Edgar Rice Burroughs could see this!*

He looked down at his watch. *Eleven-thirty already.* Hurrying back to Kori, Lou mentally went over their plan for the thousandth time. Next step: Get Kori his car.

He met Kori, assured him that Bonnie was safe. They started back to the lab buildings. From the back of Kori's lab, out on the fringe of the lighted area, they could see a lone guard patrolling slowly between the buildings. He looked bored and sleepy. But on his hip was a big pistol.

Kori looked at Lou and nodded. Then he stepped out and walked straight up toward the guard.

"Say there," he called out, "can you help me? I'm trying to get into my lab here . . . there's some work I have to do. . . ."

The guard was instantly alert. "All buildings locked. No one can enter until morning."

"Yes, I know but . . ." That's all Lou heard. He ducked around the back of the building and circled it, coming up behind the guard. He could see Kori talking intently to the guard, and the youngster resting his right hand lightly on the butt of the pistol. They were standing about ten meters from the corner of the building where Lou crouched, with the guard's back to him. Across the lighted space between the buildings, Lou could see the car they wanted.

Ten meters. Quickly and quietly, Lou slipped off his sandals, then tried to tiptoe and hurry at the same time. The sound of his bare feet on the gravel seemed deafening. The guard started to turn around.

Lou covered the last few meters with a flying leap and pinned the guard's arms to his sides while Kori clouted him across the windpipe. He gagged and went down, thrashing, with Lou on top of him. Kori calmly leaned over, pushed Lou's face out of the way, and chopped hard at the back of the guard's neck. He went limp.

Lou got to his feet, sweaty, panting. "Is he dead?"

"I doubt it," Kori said. He went to the lab door and punched the buttons of the combination lock. The door opened and the lights went on automatically.

"See?" said Kori smiling, "No alarms. I rigged them this afternoon, at the same time that I changed the lock's combination. There's some benefit to being a physicist after all."

Lou dragged the guard inside and stuffed him in a cabinet, then locked it. Meanwhile, Kori filled a tool kit with the equipment he wanted.

Wordlessly, they left the lab and re-locked the door. Then they went to the car.

"Are you sure you can handle everything by yourself?" Lou asked as Kori slid the tool kit onto the back seat.

"If you can keep them busy on the other end of the island," Kori said. He pulled the guard's pistol out of his belt. "Here. I'll get another one from the guard at the storage caves. Do you know how to use it?"

"I think so. . . ."

"It's simple. Just release this catch here and it's ready to fire. Pull the trigger and it goes off. It should have at least a couple dozen charges in it. Laser pulse does as much damage as an explosive bullet . . . like hitting something with an ultrasonic hammer."

Lou nodded and took the gun. It felt heavy in his hand.

"Very good," Kori said. "I'll wait here until you start making noise down by the harbor."

"Right." Lou tucked the gun into his waistband, then saw Kori extend his hand. He took it and said, "Good luck."

Kori grinned. "See you tomorrow."

"Yeah." *If we're both alive tomorrow.*

Lou hurried through the star-lit night down toward the harbor. The road passed Marcus' house, where the only other car on the island was parked. Lou looked around, saw no one, and then slid in behind the wheel and released the brake. The car started to roll down the slight incline and into the worn gulley of the road.

Suddenly there were footsteps behind him and a man calling, "*Wei! Li tsai tso sheng mo?*"

Lou let the car glide to a stop, slid out, and crouched down behind the car. A light came on at the front of the house. Two guards were standing in front of the place, staring at the car. Lou pulled the gun out and set the safety release.

The guards didn't seem to know he was there. They were walking slowly toward the car. Lou stood straight up and fired over the car. The gun went *crack! crack!* as hundreds of joules of electrical energy were suddenly changed to invisible pulses of infrared laser light. The first guard was bowled over backward, as if hit in the chest by a giant's fist. The second spun and sprawled on his face. Neither of them moved once they hit the ground.

His hands shaking, Lou set the safety again and tucked the gun back into his waistband. Then he forced himself to go over to the bodies and take their guns. *They're still breathing.* He felt a little better as he went back to the car and tossed their guns onto the front seat.

Five past midnight. Running late. He got in behind the wheel again. He turned on the car's headlights and saw the road running down toward the harbor. *Time for Kori's diversion.* With a deep breath, Lou turned the starter key. The turbine whined to life. Lou pressed the throttle pedal firmly down to the floor. The engine coughed, then roared. Lights went on inside the house.

He raced the engine once again, then put the car in gear and roared off down the road. The shrubs and trees by the roadside blurred by; the wind tore at his face as he plunged down the twisting road toward the harbor. Lights were going on down there, too, where the guards' living quarters were.

He came screeching out on the flat, tore into the harbor area, and pulled the car to a screaming, tire-burning, skidding stop at the foot of the lone dock. There was a small boat tied up at the end of it. The game was going to be to make it look as if he wanted to get off the island on that boat.

Men were piling out of several buildings in the darkness, shouting in languages Lou didn't understand. He went to the back of the car, lifted the engine hood and groped for the fuel feed line. He ripped it out and felt a spurt of fuel slick his fingers. Then he went back to the front seat, grabbed the two extra guns, and fired several shots into the engine compartment, backpedaling onto the dock as he did so. The third shot did it; the car erupted in flames.

Lou raced down the dock, the burning car between him and anyone who wanted to come and get him. There were a few crates piled on one side of the wooden dock, and Lou ducked behind them. In front of him was the flaming turbowagon; through the blurring heat waves of its fire he could see men running around the dockside area, some of them brandishing guns, all looking red and lurid in the light of the fire. Behind him was the open harbor, and the small boat tied up at the end of the dock.

But somebody had already thought about the boat. Lou heard a funny crunching sound, and then the crash of breaking glass. Looking over his shoulder, he saw a chunk of the boat's gunwale poof into splinters and vapor. *Laser rifle! They're breaking up the boat to keep me from using it. Maybe they think I'm on board it already.*

Then another thought: *When they find out I'm where I really am, they'll start blasting those rifles at me!*

Lou froze into a motionless, thoroughly frightened little knot of humanity, crouched behind the packing crates, trying to look totally invisible or at least as small and unnoticeable as possible. Long minutes ticked by. The fire in the car died down, the boat slid over on its side, gurgling obscenely.

Things up on dockside had quieted down. It was harder to see now, but there must have been dozens of guards milling around during the height of the blaze. Lou knew he was trapped and he was going to die. But not just yet. He realized that he had picked up a splinter in his left foot and it hurt. And his jaws ached from being clenched. He wondered how Kori was doing.

Maybe I ought to make some more noise or something, he thought. On the other hand, maybe the guards thought he had been aboard the boat and was now drowned. *If I let them know I'm here, I'm just inviting them to shoot me.*

He shook his head. *They're going to find you sooner or later, hero. Right now your job is to make enough noise to distract them from Kori.*

Squinting out into the darkness, he could barely make out a row of what looked like fuel drums lined up neatly on the shore, near the foot of the dock. A dozen drums. Maybe fifty meters away. An easy target.

It took him five shots before one of the drums burst into flame. In an instant they all went up.

Now the shouting and running began all over again. Nobody was shooting at him, either. They were all running either toward the fire or away from it. Lou watched the guards. They were good, no question of it. After the first momentary shock and surprise, they fought the raging fire with hand extinguishers, blankets, anything they could find. Finally, somebody trundled up with a portable foam generator and they started smothering the blaze with billowing white foam. But it took time, lots of time.

The fire was smoldering and smoking when Lou heard: "Christopher! I know you're out there on the dock. Give yourself up, you can't get away." Marcus' voice.

Lou almost laughed. Marcus didn't sound angry or frightened or even very upset. He was talking as calmly as the first day they'd met. That meant that he didn't realize what Kori was up to, or that Bonnie was hidden.

Or, Lou heard himself counter, *it could mean that he's got Kori and Bonnie and the whole game's lost.*

"Christopher, I don't want to have you killed. Come out now and stop this nonsense."

Like a schoolteacher scolding a kid, Lou thought.

"You can't get away, Christopher. We know you're sitting behind those packing crates. We . . ." Suddenly his voice cut off.

Lou peeked out from behind the crates. Marcus was listening to a guard who was gesturing and pointing up the road, toward the other end of the island.

"So the three of you are in on this together!" Marcus' voice sounded a little edgier now. "All right, we'll just find the other two and bring them out here. You can watch and see what happens to them."

"Marcus!" Lou called out.

Everyone at dockside froze. In the back of his mind, Lou realized that it was nearly dawn. There was enough clammy gray light to see the whole dockside area now.

"Marcus, did you ever stop to think of what a good target you make?"

Marcus jerked a step backward.

"No, don't move!" Lou yelled. "Don't any of you move. If anybody twitches, you'll get it, Marcus. I mean it!"

Marcus stood frozen at dockside. He was out in the open, the nearest guard a meter or so away, the nearest cover the burned-out hulk of the car, at least ten meters away. Lou prayed that none of them knew how many shots it would take him to hit anything at this distance.

"Christopher, you can't get away with this."

Lou grinned. "Can't I?"

As if in answer, the packing crate in front of him exploded in a deafening blast and a shower of splinters. Lou felt himself soaring, slow motion, tumbling off the dock, seeing the green land swing wildly and the greener water rushing up toward him. As he hit the water and lost consciousness, his last thought was that some rifleman had missed his head by just about a centimeter.

Chapter 18

The pain woke him up. It would have been pleasant to stay asleep, unconscious, oblivious to everything. But he hurt everywhere, like knives were being twisted under his skin.

His eyes were gummy when he tried to open them. Everything was blurred, out of focus. There was a gray expanse of ceiling over his head. And faces. He tried to raise his head, but somebody's hand pushed him back onto the pillow.

Turning his head slightly, he could make out a window off to his right. It was bright, bright enough to make him shut his eyes.

What time is it? flashed through his mind. He started to speak, but all he heard was a thick, scratchy-throated groan.

"He's conscious," said a voice.

Marcus' face slid into view. Still calm. But was that perspiration beading his brow?

"That was a foolish bit of nonsense," Marcus said without rancor. "What have you done with the girl? And where's Dr. Kori?"

Lou found the strength to shake his head.

"It's a small island, Christopher. We'll find them sooner or later."

"Not before. . . ," he croaked.

"Before what?" Marcus asked.

"Nothing."

Marcus leaned closer. "We can find out. You can't keep any secrets from us."

"Go ahead and torture me . . . it won't . . ."

"Don't be an ass," Marcus said. "There are drugs that will make you do anything."

"No . . ."

Somewhere beyond Lou's vision a door opened and footsteps clicked quickly toward his bed. A voice muttered something, too low for Lou to hear.

"What?" Marcus snapped. "Why wasn't I told sooner? When did . . ."

Marcus' face slid into view again. It was red now. With anger. Or fear? Lou smiled.

"Where's Dr. Kori? What's he doing with a bomb?"

"Planting it in your lunch."

Lou saw Marcus' hand blurring toward him but couldn't move out of the way. It stung and snapped his head to one side. He tasted blood in his mouth.

"Get him talking. And quickly," Marcus ordered.

Someone grabbed at his arm. It flamed agony. Lou saw it was red and sore with thousands of splinters from the packing case that had exploded in front of him. An expressionless Chinese doctor took his arm from the guard, held it gently, swabbed a relatively undamaged spot on the underside of the arm, and then pressed a pneumatic syringe into the area. He put Lou's arm back down on the bed carefully, then looked at his wristwatch.

"The reaction should take a few minutes," the doctor said to Marcus.

Marcus paced the room nervously. The doctor stood by the bed, patiently watching Lou. *What time is it?* Lou wondered. *How much time does Kori need?*

Somebody giggled. Lou was startled to realize it was he himself.

The doctor turned toward Marcus. "He should be ready now."

Marcus came to the bed and leaned over Lou. "All right now, Christopher. Where is Dr. Kori, and what's he doing with the bomb he stole?"

"Playing in the sand," Lou said, laughing. It was funny, everything was so funny. Marcus' face, the thought of Kori digging sand castles with a nuclear bomb tucked under his arm. The whole thing was uproariously funny.

"Listen to me!" Marcus shouted, his face red and sweaty. "Quickly, before . . ."

The flash of light was bright enough to feel on your skin. For an instant everything stopped, etched in the pitiless white light. No sound, no voices, no movement. Then the bed lifted, the window blew in with a shower of glass, a woman screamed, and a roar of ten thousand demons overpowered every other sensation.

Somebody fell across Lou's bed. The roar died away, leaving his ears aching. People started to move again through a dusty plaster haze, crunching glass underfoot. Marcus staggered up from the bed.

Lou heard somebody say in an awed voice, "Look at that . . . a real mushroom cloud, just like in the history books."

Then Lou heard his own laughter. He couldn't see Marcus, but he knew he was still there.

"You've lost, Marcus. You might as well admit it. There'll be a government inspection team here in a matter of hours. Followed by troops, if you want to fight. It's all over. You've lost."

"I can still kill you! And the girl!"

Lou was laughing uncontrollably now. *The drug,* he knew in the back of his mind. But there was nothing he could do to stop himself. "Sure, kill me. Kill everybody. That's going to help you a lot. An enormous lot."

He laughed until he passed out again.

It was pleasant to be unconscious. *Or am I dead?* But the thought brought no fear. He was floating in darkness, without pain, without anxiety, just floating in soft warm darkness. Then, after a long, long while, the darkness began to turn a little gray. It brightened slowly, like a midnight reluctantly giving way to dawn.

Bonnie's face appeared in the grayness. There were tears in her eyes, on her cheeks. "Oh, Lou . . ."

He wanted to say something, to touch her, to make her stop crying. But he couldn't move. It was as if he had no body. Then her face faded away and the darkness returned.

He heard other voices in the grayness, and once in a while the black turned gray again and he could see strange faces peering at him. He would try to talk, try to signal to them, but always the darkness closed in again.

Then, abruptly, he opened his eyes and everything was in sharp focus. He was lying in a hospital bed. The walls of his room were a pastel blue, the ceiling clean white. There were viewscreens and camera eyes in the ceiling. Lou found that he could turn his head. It hurt, but he could do it. There was a window at his left. He couldn't see out of it at this angle, but sunshine was pouring in. A night table was next to his bed, a rolling tray crammed with plastic pill bottles and syringes and other medical whatnots. A door, closed. A single plastic sling chair standing beside it.

He tried sitting up, and the bed followed his motion with an almost inaudible hum from an electric motor. Leaning back in a half-sitting position, he suddenly felt woozy.

At least I'm not dead, Lou told himself.

His body felt stiff. Looking down, he saw that his hands and arms were wrapped in bandages. So was his chest; white plastic spray from windpipe to navel. His face felt raw, as if he'd shaved with an old-fashioned razor.

The door suddenly opened and a nurse appeared. "Good day," she said with professional cheeriness.

"H . . . hello." Lou's voice was terribly hoarse; his throat felt rough.

She must be pushing forty, Lou thought. *She still looks pretty good, though.*

"How do you feel?" the nurse asked.

He considered the question for a moment. "Hungry."

She smiled. "Good! That's one condition that the automatic monitors can't record yet."

She was gone before Lou could say anything or ask any questions.

Within minutes a food tray slid out of the wall and swung over to the bed. It was clumsy, eating with bandaged hands. By the time Lou was finished, there was a knock on the door and it opened wide enough for Kori to stick his head through.

"Hi. They told me you were finally awake."

Lou's voice felt and sounded better. "Come on in. How are you? Where are we? What happened? Where's Bonnie?"

Kori grinned and pulled the chair up next to the bed. As he sat on it, he answered, "Bonnie's fine. She's here in the hospital, too, getting treated for radiation dosage. There was a considerable amount of fallout from my little toy, you know. I stayed inside a cave until the government troops arrived, but I got a touch of it, too."

"Marcus and the others?"

"They gave up without much of a fight," Kori said. "A government inspection team 'coptered to the island in four hours and eleven minutes after the blast. Inside of another two hours they had a little army of government troops covering every square centimeter of the island."

"And what happened to me?" Lou asked. "I remember trying to hold them down at the dock. Then somebody shot me and I fell into the water. Then . . ."

Kori was trying not to laugh, without being very successful at it.

"What's so funny?"

"Well, forgive me, but you are. Do you know how they found you?"

Lou shook his head.

"You were lying flat on your back in one of the bedrooms of Marcus' house. Stark naked. Sixty million splinters all over your face and body and arms and legs. And you were laughing! Laughing your head off!"

"Very funny," Lou said. "Marcus had me shot full of happy-juice, so I'd tell him where you were. So he could find you and kill you."

"I know," Kori said, still giggling. "Forgive me. It just presents an odd picture."

"Is Bonnie going to be all right?" Lou asked.

"Oh yes, certainly. She'll be visiting you herself in a day or so."

"And Marcus and his crew?"

Kori shrugged. "In jail, I suppose. The troops took them away."

Lou felt himself relax against the supporting bed. "That takes care of everybody, I guess. Oh! What about Big George? Who's taking care of him?"

Kori's face suddenly went somber. "That . . . that's the one bad part of it, Lou. . . . He's dead."

"What?"

"Somebody shot him," Kori said, his voice low. "We don't know who did it. It might have been Marcus' guards or the government troops. Bonnie was right there, and she couldn't tell who fired the shot."

"Killed him? But why?"

Shaking his head, Kori answered, "We'll never know.

There was a little fighting when the troops landed. Maybe it was just a stray shot. Or perhaps someone got frightened at the sight of the gorilla. At least he didn't suffer at all. One shot . . . he died instantly."

"Poor Georgy," Lou said.

For a long moment neither of them said anything. Then Lou asked, "Where are we, anyway?"

Kori's face didn't cheer up at all. "Back where we started. In Messina. It looks to me like we're going to be shipped up to the satellite as soon as you and Bonnie are well enough to travel. To begin our exile."

Chapter 19

The doctors made Lou stay in bed for a week, while his torn skin healed and he got his strength back. He saw Bonnie and Kori almost every day. But most of the time he lay in bed, thinking. So much had happened in so short a time. Now he could think about it, look back on it and try to fit all the fragments together, to form a coherent picture of what had suddenly happened to him and his life.

Why? he thought bitterly. *Why Big George? The main reason we tried to go against Marcus was to save George, and he was the only one that didn't get through it all right.* Lou thought of the bomb explosion and how it must have terrified the gorilla. The last few hours of his life must have been hell for such a peaceful, gentle animal. *We didn't do right by you, Georgy,* Lou said silently. *I'm sorry.*

Looking toward the future, Lou was just as bleak. They were going to exile him, of that he was sure. Kori was more optimistic, though.

"After all we've done for the government?" Kori said one afternoon, at Lou's bedside. "Risking our lives to stop Bernard's attempt at a coup? They won't exile us, they'll give us medals. You should get an award anyway; you've set a new international record for splinters."

Lou grinned with the young physicist. But inwardly, he knew the government couldn't let them go free. They would tell the world about the exile, and the government would never allow that.

There was something different about Bonnie. She was up tight, holding back something that she didn't want Lou to know. One afternoon, as they strolled together through the busy hospital corridors, he asked her.

"What's bothering you?"

She didn't seem surprised by the question. "Does it show?"

He nodded.

"I've got to make a decision," Bonnie said. Her gray eyes looked troubled, sad.

"About Kori and me?"

"In a way. You see, Lou, I'm not officially on the list of exiled persons. I can go back to Albuquerque, if I want to. Or I can go with the rest of you to the satellite."

"And stay for the rest of your life."

"Yes."

He took a deep breath.

If you married me, he said to her in his mind, *you'd have to share my exile. So I can't ask you for that. I can't even mention it.*

She was staring at him, trying to read his face, looking for something and not finding it.

Aloud, he said, "Bonnie, you might never be allowed to make that decision. You're in pretty deep with us now.

The government might decide to exile you along with Kori and me."

Bonnie stopped, right there in the corridor. "They can't do that . . . they wouldn't."

"They might," Lou said. "And if they do, it'll be my fault."

"There you are! I've been looking all over for you two!" Kori ran down the corridor, dodging between frowning nurses and muttering patients. Breathlessly, he told Lou and Bonnie, "The General Chairman . . . he's asked to see us. To talk to us. Tomorrow morning. The General Chairman!"

Lou turned to Bonnie. For the first time, he felt hope. If not for himself, then at least for her.

Despite his anger, despite his hatred of what had been done to his life, Lou felt as awed as a peasant in a palace when the three of them were ushered into the General Chairman's office. Bonnie and Kori, he saw, were also wide-eyed and silent.

The office was impressive. It covered the entire top floor of the tallest tower in Messina, stretching from the elevator doors where they stood to the sun-bright window-wall where the Chairman's old-fashioned ornate desk stood.

"Come in, come," said the little man behind that desk, in a voice cracked with age.

They walked silently across the thick carpeting, past a ten-foot globe showing the world in color and relief, complete with networks of tiny satellites orbiting around it.

The whole globe hung in mid-air, suspended magnetically. The entire office was decorated in shades of green, dark jungle greens for the most part. The furniture was all richly polished natural wood. There was a scent of orchids and other lush tropical aromas in the air. And the climate control for the big room was warm, moist, almost sticky.

"Forgive me for not rising," the Chairman said. "I suffered a slight stroke recently, and the doctors want me to exert myself as little as possible." His voice was soft, gentle, and friendly, with an undisguised Brazilian accent. He was small, slight, his bony face high-domed and haloed with wisps of white hair, his hands fragile. He was very old. His skin was white and powdery-looking, laced with networks of fine etched wrinkles.

"However," the Chairman went on, "I did very much want to meet the three of you. Please . . . sit, make yourselves comfortable. Would you like anything to drink? To eat?"

Lou shook his head as he pulled up a leather-cushioned chair. He sat between Bonnie and Kori, and the three of them faced the Chairman.

Before the silence could become awkward, the Chairman said, "I want to express my personal thanks for your courageous actions on the island. You prevented an uprising that might have taken many lives."

"We did what we had to," Lou said.

The Chairman nodded. "It must have been quite a temptation, though, to put in with Bernard's people and avoid going into exile."

Shrugging, Lou answered, "As far as I'm concerned, we *were* in exile on that island. There was no difference between the way the government has treated us and the way Bernard's people were treating us. The government was a little more polite, maybe. That's all."

"Besides," Kori added, "I think we all felt that the people running the island would be worse than the people running this government, if they got the chance."

With a smile, the Chairman said, "Thank you. It's good to know that we are not completely at the bottom of the list."

Kori grinned back at the old man.

Somehow their smiles irritated Lou. "From what you've said, it sounds like the exile is still in effect, and we're going to be shipped out to the satellite."

The Chairman's face grew somber. "Yes, I am sorry to say. If anything, this attempt by Minister Bernard to seize power proves the wisdom of the exile. Your work on genetic engineering is simply too powerful to be used politically."

"So we spend the rest of our lives in a beryllium jail!"

"What else can we do?" The Chairman waved his frail hands helplessly. "We are not monsters. We have no desire to make you suffer. We will supply you with everything you desire aboard the satellite. Anything . . ."

"Except freedom," Lou snapped.

"Regretfully true," said the Chairman. But now there was a hint of steel behind the softness of his voice. "If I must choose between the welfare of twenty billions and two thousand or so, I will choose the twenty billions. The mere knowledge that you might soon be able to control human genetics has already triggered one attempt at revolution. I will not see the world destroyed. We have worked long and hard to avert destruction from war and from famine. I am not going to permit destruction to come from a test tube or a computer. Not if I can help it."

"But what about Kori? The work of the rocket scientists doesn't really threaten the world."

"Perhaps not," the Chairman admitted. "I must confess that I didn't realize anyone except those working on genetic engineering had been sentenced to exile. Someone in the bureaucracy considers the starship scientists a threat to world stability. I must find out why. If they cannot convince me that you are a threat, Dr. Kori, then you will be released from exile and free to resume your normal life. You, and any of your colleagues who have been placed in exile."

Before Kori could say anything, Lou went on, "And Bonnie, here . . . what about her?"

She murmured, "Lou, you shouldn't . . ."

"No, I want to find out about this. Bonnie wasn't sentenced to exile. She was picked up like the rest of us, and then released. She came to the island and found out what's going on. Now where does she stand? Is she going to be shipped off with the rest of us or not?"

If the Chairman was angered by Lou's insistent questions, he didn't show it. "Miss Sterne is not a scientist nor an engineer. There is absolutely no reason for her to be exiled. Unless she wishes to accompany you, for her own personal reasons."

"You can really say that with a straight face!" Lou raged. "You can sit there and promise her freedom when you know you don't mean it!"

"Lou, what are you saying?" Bonnie reached out for his arm.

The Chairman's eyes narrowed. "Explain yourself, Mr. Christopher. Why do you call me a liar?"

Almost trembling, Lou said, "If you let Bonnie go, if you let Kori go, what's to stop them from telling the newsmen about this exile business? What's to stop them from telling the whole world? Will you want them to sign a pledge of silence, or will you do surgery on their brains? Because we both know you can't risk having them tell the world about what you've done to the scientists. . . ."

"Why not?" the Chairman asked gently.

"Why . . . why? Because the people of the world will demand that you release us. They'll want genetic engineering . . . they'll want us free. You can't throw two thousand of the world's top scientists into prison and . . ."

The Chairman silenced Lou with an upraised hand. "My brave, impetuous young man, you are completely wrong about so many things. Firstly, I do not lie. When I offer Miss Sterne her freedom, and raise the possibility of freedom for Dr. Kori, I am not lying. Why should I? Please do me the honor of granting me honest motives.

"Secondly, the people of the world already know about your exile. We have not kept it secret. There would be no way to do so, even if we desired to. You cannot whisk away so many prominent men without anyone knowing it."

"They . . . they know?"

"Of course they know. And they do not care. Do you think that the teeming billions on Earth care about a handful of scientists and engineers?" The Chairman shook his head. "No, they care about food, about jobs, about living space, about recreation and procreation."

"But genetic engineering. I thought . . ." Lou felt as if he were in a glider that was spinning out of control.

"Ah yes, your work," the Chairman said. "I admit that if you were on Earth and *showing* the world, step by step, that it could be done—then there would soon be an enormous demand for it. Catastrophic reaction. Everyone would want his next child made perfect.

"But today, you are only talking about the possibility of doing this sometime in the future. You might be successful next week, or next year, or next century. I confess that our public information experts have tried to make it sound more like next century than next week. And having you all out of the way has made the job that much easier."

"And . . . nobody cares?"

The Chairman looked truly sad. "The people are quite accustomed to talk of scientific miracles. Rarely do they see such miracles come true."

"But the food they eat, weather control, medicines, space expeditions . . ."

"All part of the normal, everyday background," said the Chairman. "Once a miracle comes true, it quickly becomes a commonplace. And the people hardly ever connect today's commonplaces with your talk of tomorrow's miracles. So your promises of genetic engineering do not excite most people. Grasping politicians, yes; hungry workers and farmers, no."

"So it's over . . . completely finished. No way around it." Lou sank back in his seat numbly.

"I am afraid so. I have lived with this problem for more than a year now, trying to find some alternative to exile. There is none. I am sorry. Somewhere, we have failed. We build gleaming technologies to turn ourselves into devils." The Chairman shook his head. "I am ashamed of myself, of the government, of the entire society. We are doing you a dreadful injustice."

"But you're going ahead and doing it," Lou muttered.

"Yes," the Chairman shot back. "That is the most terrible part of it. I hate this. But I will do it. I know you can never accept it, never agree to it, never understand why it must be done. I am sorry."

The four of them lapsed into a dismal silence.

Finally, the Chairman said, "As I told you, I will personally examine the matter of the rocket scientists. Dr. Kori, I cannot promise you your freedom, but I do promise to try."

Kori nodded and tried to look grateful but not too happy, glancing sidelong at Lou.

"And Miss Sterne," the Chairman went on, "you are free to go whenever you wish. The government will furnish you with transportation back to Albuquerque, or any place else you may desire to go. And you will be reimbursed for the troubles that you've been put to, of course."

Bonnie said, "Sir? Would it be possible for me to go to the satellite? On a temporary basis?"

Lou stared at her.

"Most of my friends are there," Bonnie said, looking straight at the Chairman and avoiding Lou's eyes. "Maybe I'd rather live there than anywhere else. But I can't tell unless I've tried it for a while."

The Chairman folded his hands on his thin chest and gazed thoughtfully at Bonnie. He looked as if he knew there was a lot more to Bonnie's request than she had stated.

"How do you think the others will feel, knowing that you can return to Earth anytime you wish to?"

Bonnie's face reddened slightly. "I . . . I would only stay for a few weeks. I'd be willing to make a final decision then."

"A few weeks," the Chairman echoed. "And then you would make a decision that would be irrevocable . . . for the rest of your life?"

She nodded slowly.

A little smile worked its way across the Chairman's wrinkled face. "I can picture Kobryn's reaction. Highly irregular. But—very well, you may have a few weeks aboard the satellite. But no more."

"Thank you!" Bonnie said. And then she turned, smiling, to Lou.

Chapter 20

It was literally another world.

Lou never saw the satellite from the outside. He, Bonnie, and Kori were tucked into a shuttle rocket that had no viewports in the cargo/passenger module. They sat in padded plastic contour chairs amidst cylinders of gas, packing crates of foodstuffs, motors, pumps, furniture. Lou swore he could hear, through the airlock that connected to a second cargo module, the bleating of a goat or sheep.

The satellite was huge, of course; a small town in orbit. From the inside it was a strange, different kind of environment. For one thing, you always walked uphill. The corridors all curved uphill, in both directions, because the satellite was built in a series of giant wheels, one within another. Most of the living quarters were in the largest, outermost wheel, where the spin force almost equaled the full gravity of Earth's surface. It took no extra physical effort to walk along the constantly uphill corridors because you didn't have to work against the spin-induced gravity. But Lou immediately resented the looks of it, hated it.

His compartment—you couldn't call it a room—was a marvel of compactness, plastic-trimmed with aluminum spray paint. Lou thought of it as a cell. An astronaut would feel comfortable in it; a scientist on duty in a satellite for a month would put up with it; Lou realized he'd be living in it for the rest of his life.

Edmond Dantes had a bigger cell than this.

Life had already settled into something of a dull routine in the plastic little world. Lou, Kori, and Bonnie were met by a greeting committee when they stepped through the airlock from the shuttle rocket. They were shown to their quarters. After he had unpacked his lone travel bag, Lou received a phone call from Mrs. Kaufman, who was acting as her husband's secretary now, asking him to meet with the Director's Council right after breakfast the following "morning."

Time, of course, was completely arbitrary aboard the satellite. So everyone ran on the same clock, set on Universal Time. When it was midnight in Greenwich, England, it was midnight aboard the satellite.

Lou spent his first "evening" prowling through the uphill corridors. He couldn't find Bonnie, didn't know where her quarters were or what her phone number was. Same thing for Kori. He could have asked someone, but instead he started walking along the main corridor. It was completely featureless, bare plastic walls broken only by bare plastic doors. All alike, except for tiny room numbers on them.

There were other people drifting through the corridors, most of them strangers, but a few men and women that he had worked with at the Institute. They nodded recognition or mumbled a hello. If they were surprised to see him, or wondered why they hadn't seen him before this, they didn't show it in any way. All Lou could see in their faces was a vague guilt, a shame at being locked up here.

Like the living dead, Lou thought of them.

The only change in the long, sloping, featureless corridor was that every ten minutes or so there was a spiral ladderway that led up toward the next wheel, in closer to the hub of the slowly spinning satellite. After passing several of them, Lou decided to go upstairs and see what was there.

The ladderway ended in another curving corridor, much like the first one, but smaller, narrower, with doors on one side only. *This left side must be an outside bulkhead.* Lou expected the gravity to be lighter in this second level, but if it was he could detect no difference. Which meant that the satellite must be much larger than he had envisioned it. He began to realize how big the satellite would have to be to hold two thousand scientists and their immediate families.

As he walked aimlessly along the corridor, he came to a section that was dimly lit. Only a few dull red light panels overhead broke the darkness; it was barely light enough to see your way along. Ahead of him, Lou saw a motionless figure. As he got closer, he recognized him.

"Greg! Hey, Greg!"

Greg Belsen jerked as if startled, then turned to see who had called him.

"Greg!" Lou said, smiling and reaching out to grab his friend's shoulder. "Boy am I glad to see you!"

"Hello, Lou," Greg said quietly. "I heard they finally got you here."

Lou's smile vanished. This wasn't the same Greg he had known at the Institute. The nerve had been taken out of him. Then he saw why Greg had been standing at this spot. There was a viewport in the wall: a small circle of heavily-tinted plastiglass. And outside that viewport hung the Earth. Rich, blue, laced with dazzling white clouds, beckoningly close, alive. It was swinging around in a slow circle, the reflex of the satellite's spinning motion.

"She's only a few hundred kilometers away," Greg said in a soft flat voice that Lou had never heard from him before. "Less than the distance between Albuquerque and Los Angeles. You could go to one of the airlocks and practically jump back home."

Lou's blood ran cold.

Lou finally met Bonnie and Kori again the following morning, after a fitful, tossing few hours of dream-filled sleep. They all arrived at the autocafeteria at about the same time, and found each other at the "menu"—actually a wall panel studded with selector buttons. Only the breakfast buttons were lit. The cafeteria could seat perhaps fifty people, at long narrow tables. It was nearly empty.

"No morning rush to work, at least," Kori said, trying to sound cheerful.

When neither Bonnie nor Lou answered him, he shrugged his bony shoulders and turned to the selector panel to study the available choices for breakfast.

"Are you supposed to meet with Kaufman and the Council this morning?" Lou asked Bonnie.

Kori answered, "Yes, at nine-thirty," while Bonnie shook her head *no*.

Surprised, Lou said to Kori, "You are? But you're not from the Institute. Why would Kaufman want you to report to him?"

"Your Dr. Kaufman has been elected head of this colony," Kori answered. "Didn't you know?"

"No, I didn't. I thought it would be Professor De-Vreis. . . ."

With a shake of his head, Kori said, "DeVreis died of a heart attack his first day here."

"Ohh." Somehow, Lou felt as if someone close to him had died. He hardly knew DeVreis, but it seemed so unfair for a man who had lived such a rich and useful life to be tossed into exile, to die here, in this place.

Kori turned back to the selector panel and tapped buttons for orange juice, eggs, muffins, sausage, and coffee. Almost immediately a part of the panel slid back to reveal a steaming tray bearing his order.

"Well," he said, "at least the food looks good."

Sure it looks good, Lou found himself thinking. *You've got a chance of getting off this jail.*

Turning to Bonnie, he asked, "Kaufman hasn't sent word to you?"

She shook her head. "No, nobody's said anything to me about meeting with the Council. I guess they're going to ignore me unless I decide to stay permanently."

Lou agreed. "Well, I'm supposed to see them at nine."

He was a few minutes late. It took him longer than he had expected to find Dr. Kaufman's office, which was in the second wheel.

It was a long and narrow room, just long enough to have a slight curve to the floor. Kaufman's desk was at one end, a long conference table at the other. All the furniture was made of plastic and light metals; it all looked temporary and cheap.

Kaufman sat at the head of the table. He had lost weight, Lou saw. There were new lines in his still-proudly handsome face. His thick hair seemed a shade whiter than it had been at the Institute. Greg Belsen, Kurtz, Sutherland, and two strangers filled all but one of the remaining chairs. Lou took the last chair, at the end of the table.

After introducing the two new faces—representatives from labs in Europe—Dr. Kaufman said, "We're all trying to accustom ourselves to our new environment. The reason for meeting with you this morning is to ask you to select some sort of project for your working hours."

"Project?" Lou asked.

"Yes," said Dr. Kaufman. "I don't believe that we should sit around and do nothing. The government won't let us have the major types of facilities that we need for our old work. . . ."

"There's no computer aboard?"

Greg almost laughed. "No computer, Lou. No big toys for any of us. No electron microscopes, no ultracentrifuges, no microsurgery equipment—nothing but early twentieth-century stuff: optical microscopes and Bunsen burners, the kinds of things you buy kids for Christmas."

Lou felt his lips press into a grim tight line.

Dr. Sutherland explained, "The government doesn't

want us to do anything more on genetic engineering. Even here. They're afraid that if we start making progress again, we'll smuggle the information back to Earth. And that's exactly what they don't want."

It all made horrible sense to Lou. "But . . . what are we supposed to do up here? Turn to rust?"

"Nothing of the sort," Kaufman said, waving his hand in a negative gesture. "We may not have modern equipment but we can still do good science. We'll simply have to be more ingenious, more inventive, and make do with the simple equipment that we're allowed to have."

Allowed to have, echoed in Lou's mind. This was a jail, no two ways about it.

"For instance," Ron Kurtz said, leaning forward on the fragile-looking table, "I've never had the time to really write up all the work I've done over the last three to four years. I've published a few little notes in the journals, but now I can sit back and write up everything carefully, the way it ought to be done."

To be published where? Lou asked silently. *In the chronicles of wasted time?*

"It's quite clear that we won't be able to make any further progress in genetic engineering," Kaufman said, taking charge of the discussion once again. "At least we won't be able to follow our previous route, which required large-scale equipment. So we're all trying to evolve ideas for useful research that can be accomplished with the laboratory equipment that we now have. We'd like you to think about what you can do, and how you can do it."

A computer engineer without a computer. Then Lou thought of Greg's elaborate lab back at the Institute, millions of dollars worth of automated chemical analysis equipment. *No wonder he's ready to jump ship.*

Aloud, he said, "Okay . . . I'll try to think up something."

He started to get up from the table.

"Oh yes," Kaufman added. "You must have some very interesting tales to tell about your adventures over the past several weeks. Maybe you'd be good enough to tell the whole population, tonight, over our closed circuit Tri-V system."

That caught Lou by surprise. "Well, I don't know . . ."

"Of course you will," Kaufman said. The discussion was ended.

Lou stood there awkwardly for a moment. Then the others started to get up. He turned and headed for the door. As he stepped out into the corridor, Greg said from just behind him:

"Don't get up tight about being a Tri-V performer, buddy."

Lou turned to him. "Easy for you to say."

Greg put an arm around Lou's shoulder and they started up the corridor together. "Don't worry, pal. All you'll have to do is sit down with me and one or two other guys and we'll talk. That's all. You won't even know the camera's on you. It's simple."

"My big chance in show business."

Greg smiled, but there was sadness in it. "Listen . . . we're all going a little crazy for something to do, something to talk about. It hasn't been easy, suddenly finding yourself cooped up in this squirrel cage. . . ."

They were heading toward the dimly-lit section of the corridor, where the outside viewport was.

Lou asked, "And what's your scientific research project for the next fifty years?"

"You don't want to see a grown man cry, do you? Weren't those guys pathetic in there? They're talking about re-doing Calvin's work on photosynthesis or writing their memoirs. Lord, they're just going to fill in some time before they curl up their toes and die."

"That would be very patriotic of them," Lou said. "The government would be awfully pleased if we all just passed away, nice and neat, without a fuss. It's exactly what they want down there."

"Hmp."

They were in the darkened part of the corridor now. Greg stopped in front of the viewport. There was Earth, swinging slowly, majestically, in rhythm to the satellite's spin.

"That's what makes it hard," Greg said, staring. "Seeing her out there. Knowing she's only a few hundred kilometers away. . . ."

Lou grabbed his arm. "Come on, snap out of it. Let's get some coffee. You going back in to talk with Kori? He's due to see the Council at nine-thirty."

Pulling himself away from the viewport, Greg said, "I know . . . but I'm not going back in there. Those guys are looking more like a morticians' convention every day. I think I'm going to go crazy . . . and soon, too."

Lou tried to laugh at him. It sounded hollow.

It was an empty day. Lou spent it prowling through the satellite's different levels, the wheels within wheels. He found a fairly decent library, a tiny auditorium, some small telescopes and other astronomical gear scattered here and there. And there was an extensive hydroponic garden running all the way along one of the smaller, innermost rings. The big event of the day was watching a shuttle rocket link up to the satellite's main airlock, at the zero-gravity hub, and unload fresh food and medical supplies.

He called Bonnie for dinner, and they went together to the cafeteria.

"Do you know where Kori is?" Bonnie asked as they put their trays down on a table.

Lou shook his head. "And I'm not going to look for him. I'd like to have you to myself for once."

She smiled at him.

They ate with very little conversation. Finally, as he toyed with a gelatin dessert, Lou burst out:

"God, this is awful! Depressing! It's just terrible. . . . How in the name of sanity are we supposed to stand it! To spend the rest of our lives like this!"

She reached out and touched his hand. "Lou . . . people are staring at you."

"Bonnie, get out of here. Tell them you want to get off on the next rocket. Don't stay. Get out while you can."

"It does look bad, Lou," she said quietly, trying to tone him down. "But it'll get better. I know it will. Right now, everybody's still sort of in shock. Nobody's used to this yet. It'll get better. . . ."

"No. It's going to get worse. I can feel it. Everybody's

so hopeless! There's no purpose to their lives, there's nothing to live for!"

"They'll adjust," Bonnie said. "So will we."

"We?"

Just then, Kori came striding into the cafeteria, long-legged, loose-jointed, and spotted them. He ambled over to their table, smiling broadly. "I've been looking every place for you."

Looking up at him, Lou snapped, "How can you be so blazing cheerful?"

Kori shrugged. "Well, I had good news for you. Greg Belsen said you'd be glad to hear it. But if you don't want me to tell you . . ."

"All right . . . all right. Sit down, wise guy." Despite himself, Lou was grinning back at Kori. "Now tell me the good news. I could use some."

"Well . . . on the shuttle rocket today they brought my holograms. The ones from *Starfarer*. Dr. Kaufman said I could show them tonight, and you won't have to talk about your glorious adventures after all."

"Great," Lou said. "Best news I've heard all day."

"Greg said you'd be pleased."

Lou walked Bonnie back to her quarters, while Kori went to find the special compartment that had been set up as a Tri-V studio.

"You can't stay here in jail." Lou told her as they walked down the corridor, "I won't let you."

"But I can't go back to Earth and know that you and Kori and the others are trapped here. I just can't, Lou."

"Do you think it'll make me feel any better knowing

that you're staying here because you feel sorry for me?"

They were at her door now. "I don't know," Bonnie said. "It's lousy no matter which way you look at it."

Lou nodded agreement.

"Would you like to come in and watch Kori's show?"

"Sure . . . I tried watching Tri-V shows beamed up from Earth for a while this afternoon. It kind of hurts; comedies and love stories and newscasts . . . all of it happening where there are cities and trees and mountains and wind and . . ."

"Stop it!" Bonnie snapped.

He looked at her. "It hurts," he said.

She put her arms around him and rested her head against his shoulder. "I know it hurts, Lou. I know."

A loudspeaker set into the ceiling broke in: "Tonight's special showing of photographs from the *Starfarer* mission will begin in five minutes."

Bonnie straightened up, looked briefly into Lou's eyes, and then turned to open her door.

They sat side by side on the sofabed, the only sittable piece of furniture in the cramped compartment, and watched the viewscreen set into the wall next to the door. They listened to Kori's voice explaining what the pictures showed, watched the stars, the myriad stars. They saw Alpha Centauri again, and focused on the fat yellow-green planet with its ice-white clouds.

Then suddenly Lou was on his feet, shouting:

"The stars! That's the way out! The stars!"

He felt as if someone had just lifted a heavy mask from his eyes.

Bonnie was standing beside him, her eyes wide with bewilderment. "Lou, what is it? What's wrong?"

He grabbed her and lifted her off her feet and kissed her.

"The stars, Bonnie! That's our escape, that's our purpose. Instead of staying here in exile, we can leave! Head for the stars! We can turn this prison into mankind's first starship!"

Chapter 21

"Flatly impossible," snapped Dr. Kaufman.

Lou was standing at the end of the conference table in Kaufman's office. Kori was sitting at his side. The members of the Council showed a full spectrum of emotions: from thoughtful skepticism to outright scorn.

"It's absolutely impossible, the most ridiculous suggestion I've ever heard," Kaufman continued.

Lou held on to his steaming temper. "Why do you say that? The scheme is physically possible."

"To turn this entire satellite into a starship? Accelerate it to the kind of velocity that *Starfarer* reached, or even more? Nonsense!"

Kori said, "With the kind of fusion engines we now know how to build, we could accelerate this pinwheel to reach Alpha Centauri in less time than it took *Starfarer*. After all, the *Starfarer* was launched nearly two generations ago, it's a primitive ship, compared to what we can do now."

"But your own pictures showed that Alpha Centauri's planets are not enough like Earth to serve as a new home for us," said Mettler, one of the Europeans on Kaufman's Council.

"You're missing the point," Lou countered. "The important thing is that Alpha Centauri has planets. Barnard's Star has planets, they've been detected from Earth. Seven of the nearest ten stars are known to have planets; one of them is bound to be enough like Earth to suit us."

"Yes, I know. But it might take you a century or two to find a fully Earth-like planet."

"Let me ask something else," Charles Sutherland said in his nasal whine. "Have you thought about the structural stresses on this satellite when you hook a fusion drive engine to it?"

Kori answered, "I've done some rough calculations. It doesn't look too bad. I'd need a computer to do the job properly, of course."

"And there's no computer here," Sutherland said, grinning sardonically. "And the government won't give us one. Neither will they give us fusion engines. So the whole scheme is meaningless."

"I think they *would* give us anything we asked for," Lou said, "if they knew they'd be getting rid of us. Permanently."

"Oh, it'll be permanent, all right. One way or the other," Sutherland said.

Kaufman frowned. "By even asking for permission to try such a stunt, we'd be telling the government that we've given up all hope of ever being reinstated on Earth. We'd be admitting that we expect to be exiled for the rest of our lives."

"Don't you expect to be here for the rest of your life?" Kurtz asked.

"No!" Kaufman slapped the table with the flat of his

hand. "I have friends who are working right now to end this nonsense. I'm sure they are. And I'm sure that they must be making some headway. And so do the other leaders from the other laboratories around the world. The government can't keep this farce going forever."

Lou shook his head. "I've talked with the General Chairman himself. There's no doubt in his mind that we're here to stay."

"He's a feeble old man. He'll be replaced soon."

"By Kobryn," said Mettler. "Who is not going to hand out any pardons."

Greg Belsen turned to Kori, sitting beside him. "You really think you can do it? Get us out to the stars?"

"Of course. It's only a question of getting the right equipment and support from Earth."

"And finding the right planet," Lou added.

"The planet needn't be exactly like Earth," Greg mused. "We could modify our children genetically, so they're physically adapted to the conditions on their new world."

"But the rest of us could never live on that world," Kaufman said.

"Mmm . . . well," Greg said, "it's just a thought; we'd still be able to make a homeworld for the children, even if we couldn't find one exactly suited for us. I think it's worth the gamble. Let's try it. If nothing else, it'll give us something substantial to work on."

"Until the government refuses to give you what you need," Kaufman muttered.

"Let's vote on it," Greg suggested.

"Now wait," said Kaufman. "Before there's any voting . . ."

But there were already three hands in the air: Greg's, Ron Kurtz's, and Mettler's. With a shrug, Tracy, the other European on the Council, added his hand. Only Kaufman and Sutherland were opposed.

Kaufman snorted. "All right. We'll look into it. Dr. Kori, you can ask your colleagues to help you with the rocketry and astronautics work." From the tone of his voice, it was clear that Kaufman expected the older rocket scientists to regard Kori as a madman.

Some of them did just that. They shook their heads and walked away from Kori, unbelieving. But a few accepted the idea. More as an amusement, perhaps, than a real possibility. But they toyed with the notion, they started jotting down notes, equations. Within a week the handful of rocket scientists and engineers aboard the satellite were all hard at work, no matter how implausible some of them thought the scheme to be. They soon took over all the desk top calculators in the satellite, watching the numbers flickering fluorescently in the viewscreens, getting more enthusiastic each day.

Greg Belsen was eager from the beginning. He started looking into the possibilities of deep-freezing people, putting them into suspended animation in cryogenic sleeping units. It was done on Earth, in rare medical emergencies, for a few days at a time. Greg wanted to put most of the satellite's seven thousand people into cryogenic sleep for decades.

"Either most of the people are going to sleep most of

the time," he told Lou, "or we have to rebuild this ship into a gingerbread house. Do you have any idea of how many megatons of food seven thousand people can eat in a century or so?"

Gradually, some of the other biochemists started working with Greg. Even a few of the geneticists let themselves be dragged into the problem, although it was well out of their field.

Within a month, Lou was asking a very suspicious government computer expert for time on high-speed computers. After a week of checking with Earth-bound scientists and government officials, the computer man allowed Lou to establish direct radio and Tri-V contact with a huge government computer in Australia.

"They're double-checking everything we do," Lou told Bonnie, "to make sure we're not slipping in any work on genetic engineering. Slows us down, but we're getting there just the same. Kori says he can't see anything to stop us. If we can get the engines built and the radiation screens, and the other equipment, that is."

Bonnie nodded at him. She had begged the authorities for more time to stay on the satellite, to help with the work Lou and the others were doing. The General Chairman himself signed the papers that let her stay indefinitely. But if Lou had really looked closely at her, he would have seen that she never smiled anymore, even though she tried to.

It took six months before they were certain. Six months of hectic work, calculations, conferences that lasted all hours, arguments, cajolings. Six months in which Lou saw

Bonnie maybe twice or three times a week, sometimes not that often. And always he talked of the work, the plans, the hopes. And she said nothing.

Then, abruptly, Lou was telling Kaufman, "There's no doubt about it. We can turn this jail into a starship. We can freeze most of the people. We can reach the stars. Now we have to get the government to give us the equipment we need."

Kaufman said reluctantly, "I'll ask for a conference with the proper authorities."

Shaking his head, Lou countered, "The General Chairman once told me that if we needed anything, we could ask him. I'm going to call him. Directly."

It was one of those moments when time seems to have snapped, and you're back in a spot where you had been months or years ago. Exactly the same place.

Lou stood in the General Chairman's office again, Bonnie and Kori beside him, as the elevator doors sighed shut. The room was unchanged. The Chairman called to them from his desk. The past six months aboard the satellite suddenly seemed like a remote and unpleasant dream. *Did I actually live aboard that plastic prison? In that artificial little world?* After a drive from the rocket field, through the green farmlands and bone-white villages, through the scented winds and steady call of the surf, through the noisy, crowded, living city—the satellite seemed totally unreal.

The Chairman listened patiently to their story, nodding and rocking in his big leather chair, steepling his fingers from time to time, even smiling once or twice. Then Lou finished talking.

For a long moment, the Chairman said nothing. Finally, "Your ingenuity amazes me, in a way. And yet, somehow, I am not truly surprised that you have come up with an amazing idea." He looked at the three of them, his dark eyes clear despite his many other signs of age.

"I will not presume to comment on why you want to leave our world entirely," the Chairman said. "I suppose that even death among the stars is preferable to you than a long life of exile." He laughed, softly, to himself. "I never expected to be faced with such a decision. I never expected that man's first attempt to reach the stars would be made under conditions such as we find ourselves in."

"Then you'll allow us to go?" Lou asked eagerly. "You'll help us, you'll give us the engines and . . ."

The Chairman silenced him with a spindly upraised finger. "You say that there are many among you who are opposed to this idea . . . many who do not wish to fly toward the stars."

"Yes," Lou admitted. "Our work to date has simply shown that it's physically possible for us to make the journey. Dr. Kaufman and many of the others—especially the older people—don't want any part of it."

The chairman sighed. "You realize, of course, that it all comes down to a question of money. Everything does, it seems. Sooner or later."

"Money?"

Nodding, the Chairman explained, "It will take billions to outfit your satellite for a journey to the stars. . . ."

"We've figured that out," Lou said. "It's expensive, but still cheaper than keeping us in orbit indefinitely. This way, you pay one big bill and we're gone. If you keep us, you'll have to feed us, doctor us, everything. . . ."

"I feel like Pharaoh arguing against Moses," the Chairman complained. "I would be perfectly willing to spend what must be spent and help you on your way, if that is what you wish. But—what of those who don't wish it? I cannot keep some of you in orbit and still spend the money necessary to send the rest of you out to the stars. It must be one or the other. It cannot be both."

"Then we'll have to vote on it," Lou said.

"Yes," said the Chairman. "I suppose you will."

So they left the Chairman's office, went back down the whispering elevator and into the car that took them back through the semitropical seaside farms of Sicily, toward the rocket field. But now the grass and sunshine and cottages were cruelties, sadistic reminders that the satellite was real and permanent and they were only visitors in this beautiful world; their prison awaited them.

They rode in the back of the open turbocar in silence, eyes wide and all senses alert to drink in every sight and sound and fragrance that had been commonplace all their lives but now were small miracles that they could never expect to experience again.

A second car followed a discreet distance behind them, and somewhere overhead a helicopter droned lazily. They were prisoners, no doubt of it.

As they got close enough to the rocket field to see the stubby shuttles standing in a row, Bonnie turned to Lou.

"You shouldn't have brought me with you today, Lou. You shouldn't have."

Surprised, "What? Why not?"

"Because I'm not as strong as you are," she said, shouting over the wind and turbine whine. "I . . . Lou, I can't leave all this, not permanently. It's bad enough in the satellite, when you can see the Earth outside the viewports. But to leave forever . . . to go out into that blackness . . . Lou, I can't do it. If they vote for going to the stars, I'll come back to Earth."

"But I thought . . ."

Even Kori, sitting on the other side of Bonnie, looked shocked.

"I'm sorry, Lou . . . I can't help it. I checked this morning. The government will still let me return, if I want to. I can't leave Earth forever, Lou. I just can't!"

"But . . . I love you, Bonnie. I can't leave without you."

She put her head down and cried.

Chapter 22

Lou sat tensely in front of the Tri-V cameras. Next to him sat Dr. Kaufman, in an identical sling chair that creaked under his weight.

They were in the special compartment that had been turned into a Tri-V studio. Everyone in the satellite was watching them as they explained their positions on Lou's starship proposal.

As Dr. Kaufman spoke in his vigorous, emphatic manner, driving points home with the accusatory thrusts of a stubby forefinger, Lou's mind was far away.

He kept seeing Bonnie's stricken face when she admitted that she would never go with him to the stars. Kept seeing the green countryside, the lemon orchards and vineyards, the safe blue sky and friendly sea that he would never visit again.

"I can't leave Earth forever, Lou. I just can't!"

Can I? he wondered. *Can any of us? Turn our backs on the whole world, on a billion years of evolution? Is that what I want them to do? Is it what I want to do?*

Dr. Kaufman was saying, "It is desperately important that we all realize exactly what is involved here. No one has ever built a manned starship. No one has even attempted to. You all know that we get supplies from Earth, every week. Even though we have closed-cycle air and water systems, we still need replenishments of air and water at least once a month.

"As long as we remain in orbit around the Earth we can get those supplies and replenishments whenever we need them. But if we leave Earth, if we try this foolhardy scheme for going to the stars, we must have air and water and food systems that are absolutely foolproof. Now, I realize that manned missions to Jupiter and Saturn have used closed-cycle systems, and they've worked quite well for periods of up to six years.

"But this star-roving we're talking about will take decades! Perhaps a century or even more! Why, none of us are even sure that a truly Earth-like planet exists out among the stars."

Kaufman shook his head, making a lock of his gray mane tumble over his forehead. "No, this star-roving idea is too risky, even on purely technical grounds. We just don't know how to build a starship. And even if the best engineers on Earth were assigned by the government to help us, we wouldn't be able to keep the ship in working order, once we left Earth. We wouldn't be able to repair it and maintain it. How many engineers are there among us? A handful. We're research scientists, not grease monkeys!"

Lou was listening with only half his mind. The other half was remorselessly reminding him: *Life is ruled by the laws of thermodynamics, just as all physical processes are. You can't get anything without paying the price. Not anything. If you want the stars, you must leave Bonnie behind. If you want Bonnie, the price is perpetual imprisonment.*

What's the difference? he asked himself. *Would it be so different, pushing this beryllium nuthouse toward the stars? We're all going to spend our lives inside this shell, wherever it's going.*

He answered himself, *Don't try to cop out. Heading for the stars gives everybody an aim, a purpose. Staying here is riding an orbital merry-go-round for the rest of your life, without hope, without anything but that big blue world hanging in front of your eyes, reminding you every minute of what's been taken away.*

"And remember," Kaufman was saying, "that as long as we stay in orbit here, there's always the chance that the government will have a change of heart, that we'll be freed. Once we break away, once we start out for the stars, there can be no turning back. It's an irrevocable step. None of us will live to see us reach our destination. Our children will age and die aboard this vehicle. Perhaps our grandchildren may find a world they can live on. Perhaps. That's a very thin hope on which to hang the lives of every man, woman, and child among us."

Kaufman stopped talking and leaned back, making the chair creak again. He turned expectantly toward Lou.

Suddenly Lou's mouth felt dry and sticky, his palms moist with perspiration. The cameras were on him now, it was his turn to speak. Should he try to convince them, or should he toss the whole idea away?

He looked past Kaufman's handsome features to the big electronic board that had been jury-rigged along the far wall of the studio. There was a light for every person aboard the satellite aged fifteen or older. When Lou finished speaking, they would all vote. A green light would show for each yes vote; a red one for each vote against the starship idea.

"You can't miss," Kori had told him before the Tri-V broadcast had started. "Most of the no votes will come from the older people, the over-thirties. But we outnumber them. I just checked the population figures."

Greg had added, "We fought like kamikazes to get them to drop the age limit down to fifteen. After all, those kids are going to spend more of their lives in this pickle jar than any of us will."

"All you need to do," Kori had said, gripping Lou's arm earnestly, "is to make a strong speech. Put it on the line for everybody. The kids will vote for going to the stars. I know they will!"

Now Lou sat there looking into the cold eyes of the cameras, but seeing Bonnie's face, hearing her voice, watching her tears.

He heard himself clear his throat. He shifted uneasily in the chair. Then he said:

"Dr. Kaufman has pointed out some of the technical risks in trying to reach the stars. He's perfectly right. It is dangerous. Nobody's done it before. I don't know— nobody knows—if we can make the engines and air pumps and water recyclers work for a century or more without fail."

Lou hesitated a moment. "Dr. Kaufman also told you that if we stay here in orbit around Earth, there's always the chance that we might win a reprieve. We might regain our freedom and be allowed to return to Earth and take up normal lives again. That's also true. It could happen."

Again he stopped, but only for the span of a heartbeat. Only long enough to call silently, agonizingly, *Bonnie . . . Bonnie . . .*

Then, "When I first came aboard this satellite, Dr. Kaufman asked me to go on Tri-V and tell you something about what had happened to me. I'm going to do that now."

And he told them. He told them about the Federal marshal and his ride to New York. Told them about the man's unhappiness at missing his family picnic. Told them of his night in New York, the gangs, the knives, the running, the terror. Told them how the Institute looked, emptied of everyone but Big George. Of his arrest, his arrival in Messina, his audience with Minister Bernard. Told them of the island, of Marcus, of what they planned to do, how they wanted to use genetic engineering and the offshoots of their biochemistry as weapons alongside an arsenal of nuclear bombs. Told them of what they did to Big George, and what they wanted to do to all mankind.

And finally he told them of the gently implacable General Chairman, of how he admitted that their exile was a horrible injustice, but could see no other course of action. And the people, the great masses of people, the twenty billions of people for whom they were being sacrificed, the people who knew of their exile but didn't care.

"This is the world we've been exiled from. A world where a few people can destroy the lives of the best scientists on the planet, along with the lives of their families. A world where savages rule the cities and civilized monsters battle to control the government."

He turned toward Kaufman. "This is the world you want to go back to! So let's assume that we're allowed to go back; let's assume that the government changes its mind and frees us. What will they do with our work? Can we trust them to use our knowledge? Can we trust them in any way? What's to stop them from exiling us again? Or quietly having us killed? Nobody cares about us. All they want is the power that our knowledge can give them. The *kindest* thing they were able to do was to exile us!"

Looking directly into the cameras, Lou said, "We have no one to turn to but ourselves. The choice is ours. We can orbit this planet, slowly dying, and hope that someday the government will allow us to return. *But do we really want to return?* I don't. I've seen that world down there, and despite all its beauty I don't want to return to it. In this universe, with all its stars and space, there's got to be some place where we can make a better world for ourselves and our children. I say we should go to the stars."

Lou collapsed back in the chair, feeling weak and trembling inside. Then the lights caught his eye. The vote shocked him: the green lights overwhelmed the few red ones.

Somewhere behind the cameras, people were laughing and clapping their hands. Somebody whistled shrilly. A door opened and Lou saw Kori and Greg heading toward him, grinning.

Lou knew that Bonnie was in her compartment. Packed and ready to leave. She was probably past tears now. Crying wouldn't help anymore. The pain won't be eased by tears, or words, or regrets.

"You're making a terrible mistake," Kaufman said, shaking his head. "Everything we need and desire is here, and you're going to force us to turn our backs on it all. You're making us leave our homes and head out into emptiness. There's nothing out there for us, Christopher. Nothing!"

Nothing, Lou thought. *Except the universe.*